SHACKLETON BLISTER
THE RUSSIAN DIARY

PHILIP CAINE

1

SHACKLETON BLISTER
THE RUSSIAN DIARY

First paperback edition printed 2020 in the United Kingdom

ISBN 9780993374883

Published by REDOAK
www.philipcaine.com
For more copies of this book, please use the website above.

Critique & Editing, Gillian Ogilvie

Cover Design, www.gonzodesign.co.uk
Cover Photo, Whitby Abbey

Printed in Great Britain

www.philipcaine.com

ABOUT THE AUTHOR

Philip's career began in hotel management and then transitioned to offshore North Sea, where he worked the boom years on Oil Rigs, Barges & Platforms. Seventeen years passed, and Philip returned to onshore projects taking a three year contract to manage accommodation bases in North & West Africa.

From Africa, Philip moved to the 'Former Soviet Union' where he directed multiple projects in Kazakhstan & Russia, a particularly exciting seven years where dealings with the KGB were an everyday event.

The end of the Iraq War in 2003 took Philip to Baghdad where, as Operations Director, he controlled the operations & management of multiple accommodation bases for the American Coalition. He left Baghdad in 2010. The last three years of his career were spent running a couple of support services companies in Dubai.

Philip's life experiences and time in Asia and the Middle East are the inspiration for his thrillers.

SHACKLETON BLISTER
The Russian Diary

Preamble

During the night of July 16th 1918, the Russian Imperial Romanov family, Tsar Nicholas II, his wife Alexandra and their five children, Olga, Tatiana, Maria, Anastasia, and Alexei, along with four loyal servants were brutally murdered by Bolsheviks.

For many years there were rumours that the Tsar's youngest daughter, the Grand Duchess Anastasia, had survived that dreadful night and vanished.

'Anastasia' did indeed disappear . . . but it was not the Grand Duchess.

Prologue

January 1917

The Grand Kremlin Palace, Moscow
Midnight

The Tsar watched as the hot liquid was poured over the heavy locks. He carefully pressed his ring into the setting wax leaving the double headed eagle, the symbol of the Romanov dynasty, glistening in the red seals.

The five large steamer trunks had been code-named after each of his children, Alexei, Olga, Tatiana, Maria, and Anastasia. Only the closest of his Majesty's retainers were present, along with a handsome young Cavalry Officer, Captain Andrei Leonid Volodin.

When the final seal was in place, his Imperial Highness Tsar Nicholas II, stood back and looked at the caskets. His voice now strained and the deep-set shadows below his eyes spoke of many sleepless nights.

'The future of our family. The future of Mother Russia lies within these coffers. Guard them well, Volodin. And may God protect you in your mission.'

The Captain dropped to one knee. 'With my honour and with my life, your Majesty.'

The heavily-laden boxes were loaded onto an old farmer's wagon and covered with straw. Captain Volodin, now in the garb of a Russian peasant, climbed aboard the rickety transport and took the reins. With a long stick he gently tapped the horse's rump. The old nag snorted and moved slowly forward, its hooves clattering on the wet cobbles.

The Tsar pulled the fur collar up around his ears, hunching his shoulders against the chill north wind. A few moments later he watched as the treasure of the Romanovs disappeared into the black Moscow night.

Chapter One

Late Spring 2019
'The South Coast of England'

Seaview Downs, is one of the most expensive residential care homes in the UK. Located on a hill above Torquay and with views over Tor Bay and out to the Channel, it is certainly not the worst place in the world to enjoy the winter of one's life.

Irina Seranova, at a hundred and one years old, was a remarkable woman. She still had all her faculties, but her inability to fend for herself was now a problem. Moving from London to the beautiful Devon coast would make what little time she had left far easier.

She'd been in residence for less than a month but had already made friends. All the residents were wealthy, so the fact she was exceedingly rich did not impress. The stories of her life in Russia, and that of her mother and father, however, did.

Irina had finished lunch and, as usual, was in her suite taking a nap. After several knocks Julie, the care assistant, slowly opened the bedroom door. 'Mrs. Seranova? Mrs. Seranova you have a visitor.'

The old lady stirred, then gingerly eased herself upright on the bed. 'A visitor?'

'Your nephew is here, madam.'

'My nephew?'

The man behind the assistant smiled and said, 'Thank you, Julie. I'll see to her now. You can go.'

As the door closed the old lady put on her spectacles. 'Who are you?'

The man was now at her bedside. He smiled, but there was no warmth in the expression.

'Hello. Irina. I'm just a friend. I'd like to ask you a couple of questions if I may?'

'Friend . . . questions . . . about what?'

'About your mother's diary, my dear.'

It was almost six-thirty. The evening meal had been underway for half an hour when Julie Lawson knocked on Irina's door and entered the room. 'Mrs. Seranova? Are you coming for dinner, madam? We have some lovely salmon this evening.' The old lady looked to be sleeping peacefully. Julie was in two minds to wake her, then noticed the colouring around the woman's lips. She went to the bedside and felt for a pulse. Nothing. 'Oh, you poor, love,' she said.

Chapter Two
'Hammersmith, London'

The old leather cover was cracked and dry but the internal pages, now yellowed with age, were all intact. Amanda Lang carefully opened the diary and read the handwritten Cyrillic. '*I was so in love with him. He was so handsome and dashing in his scarlet uniform. And when he rode on parade, I saw no other than him. I loved Andrei more than life itself.*' She looked up from the book and choked back a tear. 'That is so beautiful, so romantic.'

He nodded. 'Yeah, it is,' he said unconvincingly.

She punched his arm. 'You have no soul, Mister Shackleton Blister.'

'Ouch! I do too have a soul.'

She shook her head. 'I believe you, thousands wouldn't.'

He grinned. 'Ain't that the truth.' He tapped the diary. 'So, where did you find this?'

'I've been working on a story about this lovely old Russian lady. A really interesting woman. Some of the things she'd done. Utterly amazing. She was almost a hundred and one and rather infirm, so she'd moved into a retirement home in Devon.'

He frowned. 'Was? Had?'

'What?'

'You said, she was, and had. Past tense.'

'Yes. Yes, past tense. Irina, the old lady, is dead.'

'Dead? Not died?'

'Yes.'

'And that's why you asked me to come down. You think there's a problem with the old girl's death?'

She nodded. 'Yes . . . plus I haven't seen you for a while, of course. And I know Ruby is over in Jamaica for the next couple of months.'

'Yes, she's with her grandmother. The old girl isn't well. Plus it'll be a nice break for Ruby.'

'You will miss her.'

'We keep in touch online, but yeah, I do miss her.' He stood up and went to the big patio windows and looked out over the Thames. 'Anyway how come you have this diary?'

'I met with Irina several times; we'd become quite close. The diary actually belonged to her mother, Larisa Volodin. Irina said she had no family to pass it onto, so she told me to take it. She said I'd find a great secret in it.'

'A great secret? It all sounds a bit ditsy old lady'ish, don't you think?'

Amanda closed the diary and joined him at the window. 'She was far from ditsy, darling.
She definitely had all her marbles, that's for sure.'

He tapped the book. 'Any juicy bits in it?'

She punched his arm again.

'Ouch!'

'I haven't got through it all yet. My Russian's not bad, but the diary is handwritten so some things are not so easy to understand.'

'Right, okay. But you can understand it?'

'Pretty much, yes. Irina said her mother was a Lady in Waiting at the court of Tsar Nicholas. Irina's father, Andrei Volodin, was a Cavalry Officer. All before the

Revolution of course.' She held up the diary. 'So there'll be some really interesting things in here.'

He winked. 'And a great secret as well?'

Amanda raised her eyebrows. 'Let's hope so.'

Shack, a private detective and Amanda, a successful investigative journalist, were close friends. They had first met and worked togther in 2017, when they'd teamed up to seek justice for the killing of their respective partners.

Amanda's stylish seventh-floor penthouse overlooked the Thames. Situated just along the river from Hammersmith Bridge, the view from her balcony was one of the best in London.

Shack slid open the big patio doors and, as they stepped out onto the elegant balcony, the warm morning air washed over them. It was almost noon and the temperature was already in the low twenties. Amanda pushed the canopy button, then watched as the big blue and white awning slowly extended over the seating area.

Shack went to the handrail and looked down to the riverside-walkway. Dog walkers were out in force. He grinned at an annoyed Lycra-clad jogger as he tried to navigate the over friendly four-legged obstacles. Shack adjusted his eye-patch, then sucked in a lung full of fresh air. 'I think we're in for another scorcher of a summer, Y'Ladyship.'

No reply from Amanda.

'What d'you reckon?'

No reply.

He turned to see her engrossed in the diary. He smiled and said a little louder. 'There'll be icebergs floating up the Thames if it gets any hotter.'

She turned a page and, without looking up, said. 'Hmm.'

He went over and touched her shoulder. 'I'm gonna have a beer. You want anything, luv?'

'Hmm.'

He smiled, shook his head slightly, then went inside. A few moments later he returned with a bottle of Stella and a glass of water. The ice tinkled as he placed the tumbler on the table in front of her.

She looked up, then closed the diary. 'Oh, thank you.'

'And she's back in the room.'

'Sorry?'

He smiled and shook his head. 'Nothing.' He sat down and tapped the bottle against her glass, 'Cheers.' He took a mouthfull of beer, then wiped his lips with the back of his hand. 'Okay, Y'Ladyship, what's the plan. Why am I here?'

She put her hand on the old leather book. 'This. This is why I asked you to come.'

He took another drink. 'And?'

'And to do what you do best, darling.'

'And that is?'

'To help me find out who killed Irina . . . and why.'

Chapter Three
'Laura's Song'

The Holy Mother of Christ and All Saints, is one of the more beautiful Russian Orthodox churches in London. With its pristine white walls and sky blue dome, it could pass for a Greek structure. Inside however, there is no mistaking the classical Russian place of worship. Elaborately decorated icons cover the walls. The vaulted ceiling and central cupola are as beautifully painted as anything Michelangelo could have produced. In the centre of the elevated alter stands a large Orthodox crucifix, resplendent in the candlelight.

The priest stood in front of the altar, his scarlet and gold robes made for an impressive sight and his deep voiced chanting, in his mother tongue, gave an ethereal feel to the sacred space.

To the side, a small boy dutifully swung an ornate silver burner filling the church with the heady aroma of incense.

The mourners stood, as Borodin's Nocturn heralded the arrival of Irina's flower-covered coffin.

Shack counted those present, eleven, including himself and Amanda. He leaned close to her and whispered, 'Not much of a send-off for the old girl.'

She kicked his ankle. 'Shhhh.'

He stifled a groan and watched as the casket was gently placed on the dais. The service began. Hymns and prayers were said, then an old man moved to the front and gave a short eulogy, none of which Shack understood. Shack studied the congregation. In the front pews were six old Russians, two men and four ladies. Behind him and Amanda, three young women.

Thirty minutes passed and the service came to an end. The pallbearers returned and respectfully raised the coffin to their shoulders. The small procession to the burial site was led by the priest. His deep lyrical voice echoed around the sun-filled graveyard, as he read aloud from his bible.

'Wow,' whispered Shack, as they arrived at the grave.

A small ornately fenced-off area was watched over by a life-sized sculpture of an angel. With closed eyes and wings folded she presented a magnificent figure. Her hands rested on the hilt of a broadsword. On her chest the unmistakable double-headed eagle of the Romanov dynasty.

The casket was carefully placed over the open grave. The melodic sound of a balalaika filled the morning air. *Laura's Song*, the theme from the movie Doctor Zhivago, brought a smile to Amanda's face.

'Irina's husband is buried here,' whispered Amanda. 'They'll rest togther in the same grave.' She looked at Shack, then slipped her arm through his and smiled as he wiped a tear from his eye.

Twenty yards away, the scene was observed by a leather-clad figure, the black biker-suit incongruous in the serene graveyard. The helmet's tinted visor glinted in the sunlight and caught Shack's attention. For several seconds Shack and the figure looked at each, then the person turned and walked quickly away. A moment or two later, Shack heard the sound of a motorbike being ridden off.

Chapter Four
'Hello Again Julie'

A small reception was to be held at the home of the old Russian who'd given the eulogy. He and his wife apparently had been friends of Irina and her late husband. He'd introduced himself to Shack and Amanda as Count Oleg Stranski.

His home was in the upmarket part of Kensington, between Holland Park and Hyde Park. It was an area widely and irreverently referred to as *Londongrad,* because of the vast number of wealthy Russians who resided there.

Amanda had followed the Russian's beautiful old Bentley back to Kensington. Shack was impressed as they pulled into the driveway. The house was stylish and elegant and the Count, who spoke perfect English, was the epitome of charm and hospitality.

The interior of the house was as tasteful as the exterior, with several pieces of artwork, antiques, and classic baroque furniture.

'You have a beautiful home, sir,' said Shack. 'Thank you for inviting us.'

The old man smiled. 'Please, call me Oleg . . . Drink?'

'Yes, please, a malt if possible.'

'I have a nice thirty year old Lagavulin.'

Shack smiled. 'Perfect.'

Outside, Amanda briefly chatted and offered condolences to the Count's wife and the other three Russian ladies, then left them on the patio sipping vintage Bollinger. *No peasant-class vodka for these girls*, she thought. Back inside, she joined the three younger women. 'Hello again, Julie.'

Julie turned and smiled. 'Hello again, Miss Amanda. Nice to see you again. Shame it's under such sad circumstances.'

Amanda nodded. 'Yes. So very sad about Irina. And so sudden.'

Julie introduced the other ladies. 'This is Kathy and Susan. They work with me at *Seaview Downs*.'

Amanda shook hands. 'It's a long way to come from Devon. You must have thought a lot of her?'

'She was a lovely lady,' said Kathy.

'Yes, a lovely lady,' echoed Susan.

Amanda smiled. 'I know she had no family, so it's really thoughtful of you to come and pay your respects.'

Julie frowned. 'She had a nephew though.'

'Sorry, what?' said Amanda.

'A nephew. He came to see her the day she died.'

'She had no family, Julie. I've been doing a story on her, and I can definitely say she had no relatives here.'

Julie frowned again. 'So why did the man say he was her nephew?'

Shack joined them. 'What man?'

Amanda introduced him to the three ladies, the younger of whom blushed when she realised she was staring at Shack's eye-patch.

'What man, Julie?' he said again.

'The day Irina died . . . a guy came to visit her. He said he was her nephew.'

'Had he ever been before?' asked Shack.

17

Julie shook her head. 'Not that I know of.'

Shack swallowed the last of his scotch, then put the glass on the table. 'Can you remember what he looked like?'

'Yes. Tall, well built, mid-thirties. Nice looking. Long dark hair.'

'Could be anyone,' said Shack. 'Anything distinctive? Did he give a name?'

Julie looked at the others in the group. 'Er, actually he didn't, now I think about it.'

'Anything distinctive? Think, Julie. His clothes, jewellery, watch, rings. Tattoos.'

She smiled. 'Yes. Yes. He had tattoos,' she raised her hands. 'An ornate star on the back of his hand.'

Shack nodded. 'Well done, Julie, well done.'

'Does that mean anything?'

He smiled slightly. 'Yes, luv, it certainly means something.'

She looked pleased, then said, 'Oh . . . and he was wearing a black leather biker's suit.'

Chapter Five
'Bacon Rolls And Vodka'

The next morning it was a little after ten when the concierge called. 'Good morning, Miss Lang. There's a courier here with something for you, miss.'

'Oh, really? Okay, I'll be right down. Thank you.' She hung up and shouted to Shack, 'Just going downstairs.'

Shack was in the kitchen, knocking up a bacon roll. 'Okay. Sure you don't want anything to eat?' He heard the door close, then said. 'I guess not.'

A few minutes later Amanda was back. She entered the kitchen holding an envelope.

'You don't want anything to eat, luv?'

She shook her head. 'Just coffee, please.'

He poured her coffee, then sat down to tuck into his sandwich.

Amanda put her glasses on, then slid a finger along the embossed envelope. 'Hmm what's this?'

Shack watched as she read the letter. 'Something interesting?' he said, through a mouthful of bacon and bread.

'It's from Irina's solicitors. They want me to meet them tomorrow.'

'Right,' said Shack. He washed down the last of the sandwich with tea and continued, 'What do you think? A will reading?'

She handed him the letter. 'Not sure. Just says to be there at one o'clock tomorrow.'

Shack read the document. 'Lambert, Arnold & Associates, eh? They're one of the top firms in the city.'

'Yes, I have heard of them, darling. Legal support for the very rich and famous.'

Shack raised his eye-patch and wiped the area beneath with a napkin. 'And the decidedly dodgy as well, luv.'

* * *

Saint Katharine Docks, opposite Tower Bridge, is one of several upmarket moorings in the former docklands area of London. The dock has many facilities and is able to support various-sized craft up to sixty metres in length and, for the last few days, the biggest and most impressive vessel in the marina was the super yacht *Angelina*. At a cost of two hundred million pounds, this magnificent craft was capable of travelling anywhere in the world, while providing unbridled luxury for its twenty-six passengers.

This afternoon however, with the exception of the crew, there was only a handful of occupants on board. The owner, Konstantin Valery Mirov, his second in command Ivan Permyak, and a half dozen minders. Mirov and Permyak were lifelong friends. Both now in their fifties, they could pass for brothers. Born in the slums of Moscow, they'd survived the despair and oppression of the Communist era and, with the fall of the Soviet Union in the early nineties, the two friends were let loose on an unsuspecting world.

Konstantin, or Konni, as only his closest friends were allowed to call him, had built an international empire that incorporated oil, real estate, finance and communications. When not on the *Angelina,* his time was spent between his homes in Moscow, Saint Petersburg, Monaco or Dubai. Annoyingly for Konstantin, obtaining a permanent residence in London had, to date, presented issues.

While Konni was indeed the brains and driving force behind his vast legitimate businesses, Ivan Permyak was the person trusted to run Konstantin's shadow empire, a position relished by the ruthless and slightly mad Ivan.

The afternoon sky was cloudless and the sun warm, so Konni and Ivan moved under the shade of the rear-deck canopy. A half empty bottle of very expensive vodka rested in an ice bucket. They drank and chatted quietly, watched over from inside the elegant stateroom by two very fit-looking men. Another minder escorted a young woman onboard, seated her with his bosses, then stepped away to the stern.

'Vodka?' said Ivan.

The woman shook her head nervously.

'So,' said Konstantin, 'the babushka is in the ground.'

The woman nodded. 'Yes, sir.'

'And the diary?'

The woman lowered her eyes and shook her head again. 'I'm sorry, sir.'

The Russian stood and went to the handrail. The imposing Tower Bridge could be seen over the adjacent buildings. A police or ambulance siren screamed in the distance. 'I hate London.'

Ivan joined him and put an arm around his shoulder. He spoke quietly. 'Leave it to me, Konni. I shall fix this.' He looked at his friend's clenched fists, the knuckles white as they gripped the rail. 'Leave it to me, brother.'

Konstantin nodded, then turned to the minder and waved his hand. 'She can go.'

Ivan took out his phone and moved to the stern. He spoke quietly as Konni poured out more vodka.

On the dockside a motorcycle engine started up. Ivan looked over and saw the rider pull down the visor. The Russian smirked as the powerful machine roared off.

Chapter Six
'Very Mysterious'

Amanda spent most of the next morning reading the diary. Shack answered a few emails, two of which were to decline a couple of small enquiry jobs up in Manchester. At eleven o'clock Amanda checked Lambert & Arnold's letter again and noted their address was in Chancery Lane. Knowing Chancery was a one-way street, and parking around there a pain, she decided to book an Uber.

The taxi pulled up to the swish office building a little before quarter to one. 'Here we are folks,' said the chatty driver. 'Hope you've plenty of dosh if you're gonna deal with this lot.'

Amanda tapped her credit card on the payment screen, then handed the driver a fiver tip.

'Oh, thank you, miss, 'ave a good day an' all that.'

Shack nodded to the grinning cabbie and climbed out.

In reception they gave their names to the young man on the desk. 'Please have a seat. There'll be someone down right away.'

A few minutes later a girl stepped out of the lift. 'Miss Lang?'

Amanda and Shack stood up. 'Yes, I'm Amanda Lang.'

The girl smiled. 'Good afternoon. Would you come this way please? Miss Arnold is waiting for you.'

They got out of the lift on the top floor and followed the girl. The offices were contemporary but stylish, with polished floors, glass walls and dozens of plants. 'More plants in here than Alan Titchmarsh's green house,' said Shack.

The girl turned and smiled. 'Yes, it is rather jungle-like . . . Here we are.'

The door to a tastefully furnished office was open. The woman behind the desk stood and came forward. She offered her hand. 'Miss Lang, thank you for coming. Maxine Arnold, a pleasure to meet you.' She turned to the girl. 'Thank you, Lucy.'

Amanda shook hands. 'This is my friend, Shackleton Blister.'

The lawyer shook hands and looked at Shack's scars and eye-patch. 'You have been in the wars.' Then, the shock on her face evident, she went on. 'Oh, excuse me, I do apologise. I do tend to blurt things out on occasion.'

Shack smiled and shook his head. 'It's fine. Don't worry.'

She indicated two chairs in front of her desk. 'Yes, right . . . Please have a seat. Can I get you anything to drink? Tea, coffee, something stronger?'

Shack looked at the decanters on the side-table, then noticed Amanda's disapproving glance and shook his head. 'No thanks. I'm fine.'

'So, Miss Lang, to business.'

'Please, call me Amanda.'

Maxine smiled. 'Yes, of course . . . Amanda. Lambert and Arnold have been fortunate to represent the late Irina Seranova for many years. A rather remarkable lady, as I'm sure you'll know.'

Amanda nodded slightly.

24

The lawyer turned around in her chair and retrieved a box from the table behind. She placed it on the desk and said. 'This is for you. We were instructed to ensure you receive it. We were also instructed, should it not be possible to pass it on to you within three months, it was to be burned without being opened.'

'Very mysterious,' said Shack.

Maxine smiled. 'Indeed.'

Amanda looked at the package. An A4 printer-paper box of no intrinsic value, secured with Sellotape and bound with several strands of string. The string was fixed to the box in various places with blue sealing wax. 'She's certainly made it secure.'

Maxine slid the box across the desk. 'Well, it'd be easy enough to get into it, but I think she just wanted to make sure it was only opened by you.'

Amanda frowned and nodded again.

'And, as you see, the seals are all intact.'

'So you've no idea what's in there?' said Shack.

The lawyer shook her head. 'None.'

'Was there anything else?' said Amanda.

'No, that's it.' She passed a document and pen across the desk. 'If you would please sign for receipt, our business is done.'

As Amanda signed, Maxine touched a console on her desk. 'Lucy.'

They all stood and shook hands. 'It was a pleasure to meet you both. Lucy will show you out.'

Once outside, it only took a minute or two to hail a cab. As their taxi set off along Chancery Lane, a leather-clad figure started the engine of a powerful motorcycle, then slipped into the traffic a couple of cars behind them.

Chapter Seven
'My Dear Amanda'

It was nearly three by the time Amanda and Shack got back to her flat. They went into the kitchen and Amanda took a pair of scissors from the drawer.

'D'you want a drink, luv?' said Shack.'

'I'll have a coffee please.'

He put the kettle on then helped himself to a beer from the fridge. Amanda carefully cut the string on Irina's package then peeled off the tape. The two of them stood for a moment and looked at the box.

Shack grinned. 'Might this be the big secret the old girl was talking about?'

Amanda raised her eyebrows and took a deep breath. The kettle whistled. Shack picked it up and made her coffee. 'Here you go.'

She took a sip, then held the mug in both hands.

'Come on then, Y'Ladyship . . . open it.'

She put the mug down then eased the lid off the box. 'Oh.'

Inside was a knotted bundle of silk. Carefully she took it out and untied the knots. 'This is a Versace scarf,' she said.

Shack moved the empty carton out of the way. 'Nice.'

Amanda spread out the scarf to reveal a soft leather-bound book, several old postcards and an envelope addressed to her. She picked up the envelope and ran her finger along the flap.

Shack picked up the book and flicked through the pages. 'All in Russian,' he said.

Amanda put on her glasses and began to read the hand-written letter. '*My Dear Amanda, if you are reading this then I am dead. I have had a wonderful life with no regrets. Well, none that would worry me now. You will see in the package a book, a journal actually, that was written by my father.*

After you finish the diary, you must then read the journal. They are both important and will if you are wise enough, and I think you are, reveal the secret of Anastasia. The postcards will help you. The scarf was an afterthought. It was gifted to me by Gianni Versace himself, and I thought you may wish to have a little keepsake from me. Take care my dear and trust no one. Only God will help you in your search for the truth.
God Bless you.
Irina.'

* * *

It was almost eight o'clock when Maxine Arnold put the key in the door of her Chelsea townhouse. She'd had a long Friday, with more meetings than usual, but still hoped to get away for the weekend by six. Unfortunately the unexpected arrival of an important international client had delayed her exit. Nevertheless, getting home at that time of the evening was a bonus as she knew Anthony, her husband, would have made supper.

'I'm home,' she shouted, as she locked the front door.

No reply.

'Anthony . . . darling?' Nothing. She put her briefcase and handbag on the hallstand then dropped her car keys into the silver bowl with a clatter. The noise usually brought Jinx, her Labrador running to greet her. 'Anthony? Jinxie?'

Nothing . . . The hall clock chimed eight.

'Where is everyone?' she shouted as she entered the dining room.

The table was bare, nothing laid for supper. 'Anthony, where are, darling?' She pushed open the kitchen door . . . 'Oh my God!'

'Just relax, Maxine,' said the man in front of her.

'What the . . .'

Then came a voice from behind her. 'You heard him. Take it easy, lady.' The man behind took hold of her arms. 'Nice n' easy.'

The man in front grinned. 'That's it, just stay calm and no one needs to get hurt.' His crooked smile was incongruous as he pressed the muzzle of an automatic against Anthony's temple.

She looked at her husband and choked back a tear. His hands and feet were fixed to a chair with Gaffer tape, and a large strip was across his mouth. The front of his shirt was stained deep crimson, as drops from the gash below his left eye oozed blood.

She took a deep breath, then pulled her arm away from the guy behind. 'What the hell do you want?'

He made to grab her again, but the man with the gun, snapped, 'Leave her alone.'

She stood straight, shoulders back, defiant. 'So what do you want? Money? We don't keep much in the house, but there are watches and jewellery... take whatever you like. Just leave my husband alone.'

The man behind slapped her buttock. 'Maybe we'll take some of this.'

Maxine spun on her heels and slapped him hard across the face. The noise echoed around the big kitchen. He grabbed her again, his fist raised.

'I said leave her alone, you fucking idiot.'

She pulled loose and turned to the gunman. 'So what is it?'

He waved the weapon towards the breakfast table. 'Over here. Have a seat please, Maxine.'

She moved forward and made to touch her husband.

'He's okay,' said the gunman, 'now sit down, please. We just need you to answer a few questions.'

'Questions? About what?'

The gunman took a seat at the table. The other moved across and stood behind Anthony.

She looked at the man opposite her, thirties, fit, well dressed. Foreign, the accent probably Polish or Russian.

His crooked smile returned. 'You're holding a package. We would like that please. And the answer to a few questions.'

She shrugged her shoulders. 'Package . . . what package?'

He leaned forward and rested his hands on the table, the dark muzzle of the gun pointed at her chest. 'From the recently departed Irina Seranova.'

Chapter Eight
'Live From Chelsea'

Saturday morning saw the temperature rise again. The summer hadn't even arrived, yet the media was already talking about hosepipe bans. In the Hammersmith apartment Shack was on the balcony reading the papers. Amanda had spent most of the previous day going through the diary. This morning she tapped away on her laptop as she translated the more salient parts into English.

It was almost midday when she came out onto the balcony and handed a plastic folder to Shack. 'Here you go, partner.'

He put the paper down and took the document. He flicked through the pages, then rubbed his good eye. 'Quite a dossier?'

'A hundred and sixty pages. So you've got some reading to do, darling.'

He smiled. 'Did you find Irina's great secret then?'

She winked. 'Read the transcript, then we'll talk. I'm famished. I'm going to make some lunch. Do you want anything?'

He stood up. 'No thanks, luv, but I think it's time for a beer.'

They went into the kitchen. Shack took a seat at the counter and opened the file. Amanda passed him a bottle of Stella. 'You sure you don't want anything?'

He raised the bottle. 'No. this is fine thanks.'

A few minutes later she placed a bowl of salad, a toasted baguette and a large wedge of Ardennes pâté on the counter. She poured a glass of wine and sat down next to him. 'Mmm.'

Shack was reading but the sound, as she bit into the crunchy toast, made him look up. 'That smells good.'

'You want some?'

He shook his head and took a swallow of beer, then said, 'So Irina's father really was part of the Tsar's royal bodyguard?'

She put a napkin to her mouth and nodded.

'And her mother, a lady in waiting or something?'

Again Amanda nodded.

'Wow. Not such a ditsy old lady after all.'

She punched his arm.

'Ouch,' he stood up. 'I'm going outside. Let you have lunch in peace.'

She smeared a thick coat of pâté onto the toast. 'Thank you.'

Her tone was not lost on him and he grinned as he left the kitchen.

Fifteen minutes later she joined him on the balcony. She put another bottle of Stella on the table, then sat down with her wine. 'Interesting stuff huh?'

Shack put the file down and picked up the beer. 'Thanks, luv. Yeah, very interesting.'

She took a sip of wine. 'I'm going to start on the journal next. I've had a quick look through it, and it seems like the journal took over where the diary left off.'

Shack nodded 'Okay . . . so why the puzzled look?'

'I'm not sure yet. Still not sure why there are two separate records.'

He swallowed a mouthfull of beer, wiped his lips with the back of his hand and smiled. 'Security.'

'What?'

'Security. If you want to keep a secret, something secure, then it's safer if you have the information in more than one place. And from reading this,' he patted the file, 'Captain Andrei Leonid Volodin, Irina's dad, seemed to know what he was doing.'

She finished her wine and smiled. 'Right . . . yes. And that's why she kept the diary and the journal apart.'

Shack finished his beer, then picked up the file. 'So you need to get that journal translated pretty sharpish, Y'Ladyship.'

She stood up and flipped a mock salute. 'Yes, boss.'

As she disappeared inside, he shouted, 'Oh, by the way.'

She stuck her head out the door. 'Yes?'

He held up the empty bottle. 'You couldn't pass me another one of these could you?'

Amanda worked on the journal all day. At six-thirty she went to her room to shower and change. On her return she found Shack watching the local London news.

He pointed to the television. 'Look at this.'

Amanda came across. 'What is it?'

He nodded to the big TV on the wall. 'Look.'

One half of the screen showed a young female reporter standing across the street from a row of very elegant town houses. The building in the centre of the shot was cordoned off and a police officer stood sentry on the steps.

The caption in the corner of the screen read LIVE FROM CHELSEA. The other half of the screen showed a photo of Maxine Arnold and her husband. Amanda and Shack sat and watched as the young woman made her report.

'*Maxine Arnold, the well-known society lawyer and her husband, the eminent neuro-surgeon Anthony Goldman were found dead in their Chelsea home earlier today. The police are treating the deaths as suspicious but have, as yet, not issued any details. The victims were discovered after a neighbour found the family dog loose on the street. After trying to get a response from the house, the neighbour contacted the police. The investigation continues and we'll bring you further updates as events unfold. Now back to you, Tom, in the studio.*'

'Jesus Christ!' said Shack.

Chapter Nine
'Buona Notte'

Saturday nights were always busy at Giovanni's. The trendy bistro was only a couple of blocks from Amanda's apartment and had been a regular haunt for her and her partner, Samantha.

Giovanni no longer did any cooking, but he was always there at the reception desk to welcome customers in, and charm them on their way out. Amanda liked the old man. He would always flirt with her and Sam, even though he knew they were a couple. Samantha had been dead for over two years now, but Giovanni's was one of the few places, outside of their apartment, where Amanda missed her the most.

The bell over the door tinkled and made the old guy look up. He stood as Amanda and Shack entered. 'Mio bella cara, buona sera.'

She smiled as he kissed her hand. 'Buona sera, Gio.'

He turned to Shack. 'Signore, long time since we see you.'

'Hello again, Giovanni.'

As he led them to the small garden at the rear of the restaurant, he said, 'So, we 'ave nice table for you this evening.'

It was after eleven when Shack paid the bill and wished Giovanni good night. The old Italian, as usual, kissed Amanda on the cheeks and then her hand. 'You come back soon, mio bella cara.'

'Thank you Gio. The meal was delicious, as always. Buona notte.'

Outside, Amanda slipped her arm though Shack's as they walked slowly towards her building. 'That was nice.'

He squeezed her arm in his. 'Yeah, it was. You okay, Y'Ladyship? I know that place has a special meaning for you.'

She returned the squeeze but said nothing and walked on in silence.

They were almost at the entrance to her building when they noticed the couple in a romantic embrace. Shack smiled. 'Ah, young love,' he said quietly.

As they moved to the edge of the pavement the couple parted and stepped swiftly in front of them, blocking their way.

'What the . . .?' said Amanda.

The man moved forward, but Shack reacted first and took a swing at the guy. The punch found nothing but air as the man skilfully ducked, then came up and lunged. The headbutt split the bridge of Shack's nose, He staggered backwards, dazed. Amanda joined the fray, landing a heavy blow to the side of the assailant's face.

Shack recovered and took a boxer's stance, shoulders hunched; fists raised. 'Come on then!'

His opponent stepped back and grinned . . . as the side door of a large people carrier slid open and two more men jumped out.

Fifteen minutes after being bundled into the vehicle they came to a stop. The door was pulled open and two of the four kidnappers jumped out. 'Let's go,' said the bigger of the two.

Amanda and Shack climbed out, followed by the other man and woman. Amanda looked around and saw Tower Bridge above the adjacent buildings. 'Saint Katharine's Marina,' she whispered, before Shack was hauled away by the two men.

The man behind pushed her and said, 'Okay, lady, move it.'

As they approached the big seagoing yacht they heard music. Shack looked up and saw the illuminated name on the stern. *Angelina.*

Chapter Ten
'Two Hundred Thousand'

The party on board *Angelina* was in full swing and the large central stateroom and rear deck were packed with dozens of people dancing and drinking. Amanda and Shack were taken forward to a large office in the bow of the vessel. The four kidnappers stood and waited in silence. Shack's assailant grinned at his handywork as Shack held a tissue to his bloody nose.

The door opened and two men entered. 'Good evening, Miss Lang. Thank you for coming. My name is Konstantin Mirov.' He turned to the other man. 'And this is Ivan Permyak.'

Mirov offered his hand. Amanda glared. 'Thank you for coming?' she snapped, 'we've been abducted.'

Mirov smiled, 'Yes, I am sorry about that. Clearly my associates have been overzealous in following my instructions. And you are Shackleton Blister.'

Shack removed the tissue and a tiny trickle of blood ran down the side of his nose. 'So who the hell are you?'

Mirov frowned at the wound, then looked at his four heavies. 'Who is responsible for this?'

Shack's assailant stepped forward. Mirov snarled at him in Russian then slapped him hard across the face, the sound echoing in the confined space. More harsh words in Russian, then the four were unceremoniously ordered out.

Ivan Permyak smiled at the hired help's discomfort, as they scuttled from the room like scolded children.

Shack looked at Amanda.

The Russian turned back. 'I'll have that dressed for you.'

Shack shook his head. 'It's fine. Just tell us what you want?'

Mirov went over to a small bar. 'First I wish to apologise again.' He waved his hand graciously. 'Then I would like you to please take a seat and have a drink.'

Shack looked at Amanda again, then they both sat down.

'What can I get you?'

'I'll take a malt,' said Shack.

The Russian smiled and picked up a bottle of Glenmorangie. 'Miss Lang?'

Amanda shook her head. 'Just get on with it. What do you want?'

Mirov poured the drinks and returned to the seating area. He handed a vodka to Permyak and gave Shack his whisky. 'Nostrovia.'

'So, Miss Lang, again forgive me for the way you were brought here, but I think you will be interested in what I have to say.'

Amanda looked at Mirov, then Permyak. 'I doubt it but, as you have us at a disadvantage, what do you want?'

The Russian swallowed his vodka then nodded. 'Very well. We believe you are in possession of a book. A diary actually. Which belonged to the late Irina Seranova.'

Amanda shook her head slightly. 'Sorry I've no idea what you are talking about.'

Mirov stood up and went to the bar, returning with a bottle of vodka and the Glenmorangie. He poured

Permyak and himself another drink, then topped up Shack's glass. 'Really? You don't have such a book?'

'No. Now if there is nothing else, we would like to go.'

'One hundred thousand pounds,' said Permyak.

'What?' said Shack.

'We would like to buy the diary. One hundred thousand pounds.'

Shack swallowed the malt, then helped himself to another. 'A hundred grand? Pity we don't have it then.'

'Perhaps if I explain why we seek the book,' said Mirov.

Amanda shook her head. 'What's the point. I've told you I don't have it . . . I don't have anything from Irina Seranova.'

'Please, Miss Lang, indulge me.'

She frowned. 'Very well if we must.'

'The diary is important to us . . .'

'Us?' interrupted Shack, 'the Russian mafia?'

'I am just a businessman, Mister Blister. Not all Russians are part of the mafia.'

Shack grinned. 'Right. Whatever you say.'

'It's getting late,' said Amanda, 'can we get this over with please?'

Mirov poured another vodka. 'We are part of an organisation called *The Romanovia*.'

Shack looked at Amanda. 'Never heard of it,' she said.

'We are an organisation who were, and still are, loyal to the Romanov dynasty. We are the descendants of Tsar Nicolas's closest circle, his immortals. And Irina Seranova's diary, or rather her father's diary to be exact, is of great importance to us.'

Amanda shook her head. 'That's quite a story. But it still doesn't change the fact that I do not have it.'

'The diary can mean nothing to you,' said Permyak, 'it would be better if you allowed us to purchase it from you.'

'That sounds like a threat,' said Shack.

Mirov raised his hand in a polite gesture. 'No threat intended. But we will have the diary one way or the other . . . And why not benefit from something that means so little to you.'

Amanda stood up. 'Okay, if that's all, can we go now?'

'Two hundred thousand,' said Permyak.

Shack stood up. 'You heard the lady, guys. She doesn't know anything about this book.'

The Russians stood up. Mirov smiled. 'Very well. Perhaps you could think about our offer Miss Lang, and maybe meet with us again in a couple of days?'

Amanda sighed 'Sorry, gentlemen, you're wasting your time. Now can we please leave?'

Mirov nodded. Permyak left the room, returning a few moments later with the young woman from earlier. 'Tanya will drive you back to Hammersmith.'

Mirov handed Amanda an expensive looking business card. 'This is my private number. Please get in touch when you have thought about our offer.'

She slipped the card in her bag. 'Now can we go?'

'Of course . . . Dasvidanya.'

'Just a second,' said Shack, then he picked up the glass and finished off his drink. 'Night, gents, enjoy your party.'

Chapter Eleven
'Count Stranski Is Here'

It was well after one o'clock by the time they got back to Amanda's. The night had been eventful to say the least and the meeting with the Russians decidedly worrying. Nothing was said in the car or indeed until they got into the flat.

Amanda flopped down on the couch. 'Well, partner, what do you make of that?'

He went towards the kitchen. 'D'you want anything?'

She shook her head.

'I'm gonna have a nightcap. Be right back.'

A few moments later he returned with a glass of whisky and sat down beside her.

She slipped her arm through his. 'So, detective . . . What do you think?'

Shack swallowed half his drink. 'I think they're pretty dangerous. But, something's not right.'

'Go on.'

'Why would they offer to actually buy the diary? Usually your average Russian villains are pretty much the 'wild bunch' and just take whatever they want.'

Amanda nodded. 'Yes, you're right. But maybe these guys are a little more subtle?'

He finished off the scotch and put the glass on the table. 'Subtle, eh?'

She gave a little smile. 'Well, you know what I mean.'

He sat up straight, then said, 'They never mentioned the journal.'

'No.'

'All they were interest in was the diary.'

She nodded. 'Yes. Which could mean one of two things. One, that what they want is in the diary and they don't care about the journal. Or two, they just don't know about the journal.'

'How're you getting on with the translation?'

'I'll get it finished tomorrow.'

'Okay, good. Then we can see exactly what these two books mean.'

She smiled again. 'I think I know. But I'll wait until you read the transcript and see what you think.'

He stood up and offered his hand. 'Okay, Y'Ladyship, time for bed.'

She took his hand and stood, then gave him a peck on the cheek. 'Night, partner.'

* * *

The following morning Amanda was in the kitchen, making tea, when the house phone rang. 'Hello?'

'Good morning, Miss Lang. There's a gentleman here to see you, Miss.'

'Morning. Who is it please?'

'He said his name is Oleg Stranski, Miss.'

'Oh . . . Right. Ask him to come up please.'

'Yes, Miss.'

She put the tea things on a tray, added an extra mug, then went into the lounge. 'Oleg Stranski is here.'

Shack was on his laptop answering emails. 'What?'

'Count Stranski . . . he's here.'

Shack closed the laptop and went across to her. 'Really? Now what does he want?'

The doorbell chimed. She put the tray down. 'I guess we're about to find out.'

Shack opened the door. 'Count Stranski, Oleg. Good morning.'

The old Russian smiled. 'Good morning. Please excuse this unannounced intrusion on such a lovely Sunday morning.'

'Not at all,' said Amanda, 'please come in. Would you like some tea?'

The old man nodded. 'Thank you.'

Tea poured, Amanda said, 'So, what can we do for you, Oleg?'

Stranski took out a handkerchief, coughed and cleared his throat. 'Excuse me.'

Shack smiled at the dapper old gent.

'I shall come straight to the point, my dears. I believe you were aboard the *Angelina* last night. And met with Konstantin Mirov.'

Shack and Amanda looked at the old Russian. He smiled at the look on their faces.

'And you know this, how?' said Shack.

'I may be old but, I believe the saying is, I still have a finger on the pulse.'

'That still doesn't tell us how you know we were there, Oleg,' said Amanda.

'Don't worry, my dear, there is nothing sinister. There happened to be a couple of my associates at the party. They saw you arrive with Mirov's men. And you were somewhat worse for wear, my dear Shack.'

Shack touched the wound across his nose. 'Yeah. A little altercation with one of them.'

'Can I ask what he wanted?'

'Why are you interested, Oleg?' said Amanda.

'Please, indulge me. What did he want?'

'He wanted to know if I had a book, a diary actually.'

'And do you have this diary, my dear?'

Amanda shook her head, then took a sip of tea. 'No . . . I had no idea what he was talking about.'

'Did he say who's diary this was?'

'He said it was your friend Irina's father's.' said Shack.

The old boy nodded. 'Yes, all right . . . But you don't have the book?'

'Oleg, I'm not sure what this is all about and I certainly don't understand why everyone seems to think I have this damn diary.'

The Russian raised his hand. 'Please calm yourself, my dear. I apologise if I've upset you.'

'I'm not upset, I just don't understand what all the fuss is about this book.'

The three sat in silence for a moment and finished their tea. Then the Russian said, 'Did he say why he wanted the book, the diary?'

Shack nodded. 'Said it was important to them.'

'Them?'

'Yes. He said he, they, were part of some loyal society to the old Tsar. And the diary was important to them.' Shack shrugged his shoulders. 'Or something like that.'

The old man smiled. 'Did he now? And was this loyal society, *The Romanovia*?'

They both looked at Oleg and said in unison, 'Yes.'

Again he smiled. 'He really is a fox, our Mister Mirov.'

'So, you obviously know of this *Romanovia* then?' said Amanda.

'I do indeed, my dear and I can say with all certainty, that Konstantin Valery Mirov has nothing to do with us.'

'Us?' said Shack.

'Yes . . . us. Because I belong to *The Romanovia*.'

Chapter Twelve
'Down to Devon'

After Count Oleg had left, Amanda said, 'What do you make of that, partner?'

'Seems like everyone is looking for the old girl's diary.'

'It does, and it's hard to know what to do next. Especially when Irina's letter said to trust no one.'

'Well I'm gonna get another cuppa, then I'll finish reading the diary transcript.'

'Okay. I've almost finished translating the journal. Another couple of hours and it should be done.'

'Good . . . it'll give me something to read on the way to Devon.'

'We're going to Devon?'

'We are, Y'Ladyship. I think it's about time we had a good chat with the three girls who were at Irina's funeral.'

'Why?'

'Not sure yet, but something's not right about the day the old lady died.'

'Sounds like a plan. Maybe stay over as well? It's quite a drive.'

'Okay, if you like. I'll book a couple of rooms.'

'Maybe just get a twin? No need for two.'

'Really? '

'Of course. A twin will do fine, partner.'

* * *

The Sunday traffic in the city was not as horrendous as usual, and they hit the M3 ten minutes after leaving Hammersmith. The motorway heading south west was busy, but fast flowing and they made good time. Shack spent the first couple of hours reading Amanda's transcript of Volodin's journal but dozed off for the last hour or so.

It was a few minutes after five when the Evoque pulled into *Seaview Downs* visitor's parking.

Inside, Amanda recognised the lady at the Reception Desk. 'Good afternoon, Mary.'

'Oh, good afternoon, Miss Lang. Nice to see you again.'

Amanda smiled. 'Yes, you too.'

The receptionist looked at the one-eye man, and said, 'Good afternoon, sir,' then turned back to Amanda. 'So sad about Mrs. Seranova.'

'Yes, it came as quite a shock. So sudden.'

'Are you visiting another resident today, Miss?'

'Actually no. We've come down from London to have a chat with Julie.'

Mary stood up. 'Oh . . . Julie? Er, would you mind having a seat for a second, please. I'll just get the director.'

Shack turned to Amanda and frowned. 'What's that all about?'

A few minutes later Mary returned with another woman. 'This is Mrs. Thomson, our facility director. This is Miss Lang.'

Shack held back as Amanda and the director shook hands. 'Hello.'

Thomson gave a little smile. 'Hello, Miss Lang. I believe you were a friend of the late Mrs. Seranova?'

'Yes, that's right.'

'My condolences.'

Amanda nodded. 'Thank you . . . As I've just told Mary, we've travelled from London to talk to Julie . . . if that's convenient?'

The director touched Amanda's arm. 'Let's move out of reception.' They entered a small side-room. 'Please, have a seat.'

The three sat down. 'Is there a problem, Mrs. Thomson?' said Amanda.

The woman was silent for a few seconds, then took a deep breath. 'I'm afraid Julie died two days ago.'

'Died!' said Shack.

The director turned to him and nodded.

Amanda slumped back in her chair. 'But we were only with her a few days ago, at Irina's funeral.'

Shack stood up. 'How did she die?'

The woman took a tissue from her skirt pocket and wiped her nose. 'Please, excuse me. We see death here quite regularly, as I'm sure you'll appreciate. But when a young woman like Julie . . .'

Amanda put a hand on Thomson's arm. 'It's alright . . . It's alright.'

Again Shack asked, 'How did she die, Mrs. Thomson?'

'An awful accident. She fell from the cliffs.'

Shack looked at Amanda, then turned to the director. 'Could we speak to the other ladies. Kathy and Susan?'

'Not just now. They've taken a couple of days off. They were terribly upset. They were all so close.'

He nodded. 'I understand, but it'd be helpful if we could talk to them, please?'

She sniffed and wiped her nose again. 'It's not usual for us to give out staff details, sir.'

'Mrs. Thomson, this is really important. Could you call Kathy and Susan . . . ask if we could meet with them please?'

The director got up. 'Very well. I'll be back shortly.'

As the door closed, Shack frowned and looked at Amanda. 'An accident?'

She stood up. 'Let's just talk to the girls first. See what they have to say.'

Thomson returned. 'Okay, Kathy and Sue said they'd speak to you. Here's their address.'

Shack looked at the paper. 'Just one address?'

She nodded. 'Yes. They all share a house in town.'

Amanda smiled. 'Thank you, Mrs. Thomson, you've been very helpful.'

Shack held up the paper. 'Thanks for this. Take care.'

The director opened the door. 'Have a safe trip back to London.'

'We're staying over actually, going back in the morning.'

'Ah, well, in that case enjoy Torquay . . . Goodbye.'

As they drove away, Thomson took out her phone and tapped out a WhatsApp message . . .

A woman called Amanda Lang was just here.

What did she want?

Wanted to talk to Julie.

Was she alone?

With a one-eyed man. They've gone to talk to two of the staff.
Anything else?
They're staying down here.
Are they now - until when?
Tomorrow.
Okay.

Chapter Thirteen
'Kathy & Susan'

It was only a short drive from *Seaview* down into Torquay. They passed through the busy harbour area and out to the suburbs west of town. The house they were looking for was in a row of old fisherman's cottages. Amanda pulled up in front of the last cottage.

As they got out, the front door opened, and Kathy appeared. She raised her hand and smiled. 'You found us.'

Amanda waved back. 'Hi, yes.'

Shack opened the gate and held it for Amanda. 'Thank you for seeing us, Kathy. We're so sorry about Julie.'

'Yes . . . thank you. Please, come in. We're in the back garden.'

Susan stood up as the three came out of the house.

'Hi, Susan, sorry to bother you.' said Amanda.

'It's fine. Can we get you anything? Tea? A cold drink?'

'No, thanks,' said Shack, 'we won't keep you. Just need to talk to you about Julie if that's okay?'

They sat down under the shade of a large parasol. Shack studied the two girls as Amanda spoke.

'Mrs. Thomson said Julie fell from the cliffs, ' said Amanda.

The girls nodded.

'Do you know how that happened? Have the police said anything?'

Kathy picked up her glass and took a sip. 'They said she was jogging and must have stumbled or something near the edge.'

Amanda leaned forward onto the table. 'Did she jog a lot?'

Susan nodded. 'Yes. Before or after her shift usually. At least three times a week.'

'The same route?' said Shack.

Kathy shook her head. 'Not sure. We never went with her.'

Shack gave a smile. 'Right.'

'This must be an incredibly sad time,' said Amanda. 'Irina passing and now this awful accident with Julie.'

Kathy nodded. 'Yes, we were only starting to get to know her.'

'Irina?' said Shack.

Kathy moved a little further under the shade. 'Her too, I suppose. But I meant Julie.'

Shack frowned. 'Julie? I got the impression you guys had worked together for some time.'

Susan shook her head. 'No, no. Julie has only been here . . . was only here, for a few weeks.'

Kathy took another drink. 'She came a couple of days after Irina, Mrs. Seranova arrived.'

'Really?' said Amanda.

Susan nodded. 'Yes. Mrs. Seranova arrived four weeks past Friday and Julie started on the Monday I think.' She looked at Kathy. 'That's right isn't it?'

'Yeah, I think so.'

There was silence for a few moments, then Shack said, 'Would you mind if we had a look in her room?'

The girls looked at each other. 'Why?' said Susan.

'We've been asked to follow-up on the accident by Julie's parents. Maybe there's something that could help us.'

The girls looked at each other again. 'Okay, suppose so,' said Kathy. 'We were going to pack her things ready for her father to collect anyway.'

Shack smiled. 'Oh . . . He's been in touch then?'

Kathy nodded. 'Yes. Mrs. Thomson contacted her parents the day of the accident. They'll be here tomorrow.'

Shack glanced at Amanda, then stood up. 'Right, ladies. So if we could have a quick look at her room, we'll be out of your hair.'

The girls stood up. 'Yeah sure,' said Kathy.

Fifteen minutes later, Susan and Kathy waved from the front door as Amanda's car pulled away.

As she turned onto the main road she said, 'We've been asked to check it out by her parents. Really? . . . That was the best you could come up with?'

Shack shrugged. 'We had to get into her room didn't we?'

'What if she didn't have any parents?'

'Everyone has parents, luv.'

'You know what I mean, they could have been dead or something.'

He winked. 'Good job they're not then, eh?'

Amanda shook her head. 'Oh well, it worked anyway.'

Shack leaned across and gave her a peck on the cheek. 'Right, Y'Ladyship. Hotel. Shower. Beer. And not necessarily in that order.'

Chapter Fourteen
'Bad News'

The Grand Hotel, on the Torquay Esplanade, is probably the smartest hotel in town. With a view over Tor Bay and the park adjacent, its location is second to none.

'Welcome to the Grand Hotel, sir, madam. What name is it, please?' asked the receptionist.

'Blister,' said Shack, 'I booked a twin.'

The receptionist smiled. 'I have a nice twin overlooking the park, sir?'

Shack handed over his credit card. 'That'll do nicely, thank you.'

'Will you need a dinner reservation, sir?'

Shack turned to Amanda. 'You want to eat here?'

'Sure, why not.'

Shack took his card back. 'How about eightish?'

The receptionist nodded. 'Very good sir, that's booked for you.' He handed over two key-cards. 'Third floor, 301, sir. Enjoy your stay.'

As they walked away from the desk Shack said, 'Fancy a quick drink before we go up?'

She shook her head. 'You go and have a beer. I need a shower. I'll see you up there.'

He handed her one of the key-cards. 'Okay, I'll be up shortly.'

By seven-forty they'd both showered and changed and, after a quick drink in the bar, entered the restaurant. The Maître d' greeted them. 'Good evening, sir, madam.'

'We have a table for eight, but we're a little early,' said Shack.

'No problem, sir. Would you like to eat inside or out?'

Shack turned to Amanda. 'Outside would be nice.' she said.

A few moments later they were seated at the edge of the elegant terrace, overlooking Tor Bay. Another waiter arrived and took drinks orders.

They perused the menu. 'So, what d'you think, Y'Ladyship?'

'Hmm . . . not sure, maybe salmon.'

'Not the food, luv.'

She looked up. 'Ah, you mean Julie?'

He put his menu down as their drinks arrived. The waiter left and Shack picked up his beer. 'Cheers. I need this.' He swallowed half the pint, then said, 'Yeah . . . Julie.'

It was almost ten-thirty when the lift doors opened. An older couple smiled as they stepped out, the lady clearly surprised at the sight of the man with the eye-patch. Shack held the door back as Amanda entered. 'Been a long day,' she said.

He nodded as the door slid shut. 'Yeah, and a lot to think about. When we get back we'll go through the diary and the journal transcripts together. Irina, Julie, Maxine Arnold. All linked to those bloody books.'

Amanda nodded as the lift pinged and the doors slid open. She linked her arm through his as they walked along to their room. Shack swiped the key-card, just as her phone beeped.

She didn't recognise the number but swiped the screen. 'Hello?'

'Good evening, is that, Miss Amanda Lang?'

'Yes.'

'This is DC Peers, Miss. Hammersmith Police. I'm afraid a have some bad news.'

'Is it my father?'

'Oh no, Miss . . . nothing like that. It's your apartment. There's been a break-in.'

'A break-in?'

'Well. I say break-in, the flat was actually accessed using your entry-code.'

'I don't understand?'

'Will you be home any time soon, Miss Lang?'

'I'm in Devon. Won't be back until tomorrow morning.'

'Ah, okay.'

'I don't understand, detective, how anyone could get in with our building security?'

'They got your code from the Concierge, Miss.'

'I'm sorry. How's that possible?'

'They gave him a bit of a slap, Miss. Forced him to give up your access-code.'

'Oh, no. Was it George? Is he alright?'

'He's fine. A few cuts and bruises. They've taken him to hospital. Apparently the old guy wasn't going to help them, but they cut-up a bit rough.'

'And my flat? Is it bad?'

'Just a second, I'll switch on Facetime.'

Shack closed and locked the door, then turned to Amanda. 'What the hell is . . .?'

She raised her hand and whispered, 'Just a second.' She turned the phone so he could see the screen.

The young detective's face filled the frame, then the view turned to the interior of the flat. As he live-fed the scene, he said. 'I have to say, Miss Lang, this is the tidiest burglary I've ever seen.'

Amanda and Shack watched as the detective moved through the flat. Each room was as undisturbed, or undamaged, as the previous. 'Obviously I don't know if anything has been taken, but there's no mess at all.' The screen was filled with the detective's face again. 'So you'll be back tomorrow, Miss Lang?'

'Yes.'

'Okay . . . I'll come back and see you on Tuesday morning. That will give you time to check the place over, Miss.'

'Okay, thank you. Can the door be secured?'

'Yes, yes it's fine. I'll close it on my way out.'

'Thank you, Detective Peers. See you on Tuesday.'

'Good evening, Miss.'

Chapter Fifteen
'Old George'

Monday morning's traffic was a lot busier than the previous day and the journey back to London took over four hours. It was after midday when Amanda pulled into her parking space in Hammersmith. They took the lift from the basement carpark up to the ground floor reception and stepped out. Amanda went straight to the reception desk. George, the Concierge, was behind the counter.

'Oh, my goodness, George. How are you?'

'Afternoon, Miss Lang. Not too bad, thank you, Miss.'

Shack looked at the old guy. 'You've been in the wars, mate?'

George grinned, then winced as he put a hand up to his face. The skin around his left eye was badly discoloured and swollen, with a neat row of surgical sutures above the eyebrow. And with the large bruise along the jawline, he looked more like a boxer than an in-house concierge.

'It's worse than it looks, Sir. A couple of stitches and a few bruises.'

With obvious concern in her voice, Amanda said, 'What on earth are you doing in work?'

'I'm fine, Miss . . . really. Got checked out at A and E last night. Nothing to worry about.'

'You feel like talking about it, George?' asked Shack.

The Concierge shrugged. 'Not a lot to say really, Sir. Three blokes came in. Forced me into the back office. Said they wanted the access-code for your apartment,

Miss. When I refused they laid into me. Taped me to the chair and said they were gonna' start cutting off me fingers.'

Amanda grimaced. 'Oh my God, George.'

'I'm afraid that's when I gave 'em the password for the computer . . .told 'em where all the apartment key-codes were . . . sorry, Miss.'

'What happened next?' said Shack.

'One of them stayed with me in the back, the other two went up the flat.'

Shack nodded. 'Go on, mate, you're doing great.'

'That's it really. They were back down in about ten minutes. Then they buggered off. Left me tied up in the back. Tom, the other Concierge, came on shift at ten o'clock and found me. Called the cops and an ambulance. Like I said, not much to tell at all.'

'Can you describe the bastards?' said Shack.

The old boy grinned at Shack's profanity. 'All looked the same, Sir. Early thirties. Fit. Black coveralls, baseball caps and gloves.'

Shack nodded. 'Accent?'

'Definitely Russian.'

'You're sure?' said Amanda.

'Yes, Miss. For sure. There's plenty of em' in London. I know that accent.'

Shack smiled. 'What about CCTV?'

'Yes, sir, it must have all been on camera. I guess that copper . . . sorry, I mean the detective that was here last night, will probably have taken a download.'

Shack offered his hand. As they shook, he said, 'Thanks, George, you've been really helpful.'

Amanda smiled. 'I hope you feel better soon, but I still think you should be at home.'

The old boy winked. 'Nah . . . I'd only get fussed over by the wife, Miss.'

Chapter Sixteen
'Whispers'

Amanda and Shack took the lift to the top floor. At her apartment door she hesitated before entering the key-code.

'You okay, luv?' said Shack.

She nodded. 'Yes . . . yes I'm fine, just got a strange feeling for a second. Just being silly.' She tapped-in the code and opened the door, waited a few seconds then programmed a new entry code. Shack watched as the numbers were confirmed on the tiny display.

They entered, closed the door, and looked around the room in silence. Nothing appeared to be out of place. The papers from Sunday morning were still on the couch. A few fallen petals from a vase of tulips lay on the side table.

Amanda took a deep breath, then let out a sigh. 'Tea first, then I'll have a good look around.'

He took her bag. 'Sit down, Y'Ladyship. I'll put the kettle on.' He went into the bedrooms, left their bags, and returned a few moments later. 'Let's get a bit of fresh air first.'

She frowned. 'What?'

He slid open the patio doors and stepped out. 'Come on then.'

She got up and frowned again. 'I thought we were having tea?'

Shack leaned on the hand-rail and looked out over the Thames. As she joined him he raised a finger to his lips.

Then made a big deal of pointing across the river. 'What do you think of that?'

She looked towards the far bank at nothing in particular.

He moved closer and whispered. 'I think I've got it. The reason they were here.'

She leaned on the rail, shoulder to shoulder with him and whispered. 'What?'

'The flat hasn't been turned over. Okay, there could still be something missing, but we'll find that out soon enough. And if they were looking for the diary, the place would have been ransacked.'

She nodded.

'So they're either sending a message or . . .'

'What message?'

'That they can get to us anywhere.'

She nodded again. 'Or?'

He turned and looked at her. 'They've bugged the place. They were only here five or six minutes. Doesn't take long to plant a couple of devices.'

'You think?'

He nodded.

'So what do we do?'

'Go back in. Make the tea. I'm going out for a few minutes to make a call. When I come back, we don't mention the diary; Irina, or Devon . . . Okay?'

'Okay.'

Out in the corridor Shack swiped through the contacts on his phone, tapped one and waited for several seconds.

'Hello.'

He cleared his throat. 'Raymond, hello. It's Bobby.'

'Bobby . . . Bloody hell, haven't heard from you for God knows how long.'

'Yea, sorry . . . it's been a while.'

'Everything okay, Bobby?'

'Er, yeah, kind of. Listen, Ray, I need you to do something, mate.' A few minutes later Shack tapped in the new access code and went back inside. 'Hey, forget the tea. I could do with a beer. Let's go get some lunch.'

Chapter Seventeen
'Raymond'

It was almost five-thirty when Shack saw Raymond enter the *Seven Keys*. He stood up and waved as Ray eased his way through the busy West End boozer.

The two men hugged. Shack smiled. 'Great to see you again, mate. You look well.'

'You too, Bobby. Been a while.'

Amanda stood up. Shack said, 'Ray, this is my good friend Amanda. Amanda, this is my brother-in-law, Raymond.' They shook hands and Shack continued. 'Can I get you a drink?'

'Bottle of lager, please.'

'Okay.' He turned to Amanda. 'You want another, luv?'

She waved her hand slightly and shook her head.

'Be right back, guys.'

As they sat down, Amanda smiled. 'I didn't know Shack had a brother-in-law.'

Ray put the case he was carrying under the table, then frowned. 'Shack?'

'Ah . . . yes. You'll probably still know him as Bobby Stone.'

Raymond's frown remained. 'Yes. Yes, I do. But now I think about it, I remember reading in the paper. Er, must be over a year now . . . the court case. He was exonerated. The accident, when Chrissy was killed, he was set up. All that carry on with the corrupt police. They really stuck it to him. Yes, I remember he changed his name when he came out of prison . . . Shackleton something?'

Shack put the drinks on the table. 'Blister.'

Ray looked up and grinned. 'Shackleton Blister. That's some moniker.'

Shack sat down and tapped his pint against Ray's bottle, 'Cheers, bro. Good to see you again.'

The big man smiled, 'Cheers Bobby . . . Shack . . . what do I call you?'

'Shack's fine, mate.'

Raymond pointed to Shack's face. 'And the eye? What happened there?'

Shack instinctively adjusted the patch. 'A little memento from the Scrubs.'

Ray shook his. 'Yeah, they really did stick it to you.'

Amanda took a sip of wine, then looked at Shack. 'So, now we're all here. Do you mind telling me what's going on?'

He swallowed a mouthful of beer, then leaned a little closer to her. 'As I said, Raymond here was my wife's brother.'

At the mention of his dead wife, Shack lowered his head and became silent. Several seconds past, then Amanda touched his hand. 'Go on, partner.'

'Yeah, sorry.' Shack spoke quietly and continued. 'Ray works for Special Branch.'

Raymond looked at Amanda and smiled. 'I'm only in the tech department, so nothing too exciting.'

'I had him sweep the apartment this afternoon.'

The big man picked up his briefcase and placed it on the seat next to him. He glanced around the busy bar; no one was paying them any attention. He flicked open the locks and reached inside, then placed two small gadgets on the table in front of Shack. 'Found these in the lounge and kitchen.'

Shack turned one over in his hands. 'Surveillance cameras?'

Ray took a swig of beer, then nodded. 'Sound and vision. High powered. Movement activated. Burst transmission.'

Amanda picked one up. 'Not your usual front door cameras from Amazon then?'

Ray shook his head slightly. 'This is military grade technology.'

Shack looked at his brother-in-law. 'Whose military?'

Ray leaned forward. 'Russian, GRU.'

'GRU!' said Amanda, 'Russian Military Intelligence, bugged my flat?'

'Maybe not them 'per se' but that equipment is definitely GRU issue.'

Shack spun the little camera around on the table. 'So you'd have to be pretty well connected to get hold of this gear?'

Raymond shook his head. 'Not necessarily. Nowadays, in Russia, you can get hold of anything if you have the money.'

Shack grinned. 'Ain't that the truth.'

Ray finished his beer then sat back in his seat. 'So, what's this all about, Bobby . . . Shack? What've you got yourself into, bro?'

Chapter Eighteen
'Bolshoi Tonight'

Outside the *Seven Keys,* Shack hugged Raymond. 'D'you think you could you drop Amanda home, please?'

'Sure, but where're you off to?'

Amanda frowned. 'Yes, where are you going?'

Shack winked. 'I won't be long, maybe an hour or so. I'll get a cab and see you back at your place.'

She shook her head slightly, the frown still there. 'Okay.'

Shack turned to his brother-in-law. 'Thanks again, Ray. I'll be in touch mate.'

As they walked away, Shack stepped into the road and flagged down an approaching black-cab.

Twenty minutes later the taxi came to a stop. 'Seventeen-fifty, sir.' said the driver.

Shack handed over a twenty. 'Keep the change mate.'

The cabbie smiled. 'Cheers,' and looked up at the gleaming yacht, 'oh, nice one.'

Shack nodded then walked to the gangway. As he stepped on to it a figure appeared at the top. Shack continued forward.

The man held up his hand but before he could speak a woman appeared. 'Niet problem, Grigori,' she smiled at Shack. 'This way, sir.'

Grigori stepped aside. Shack winked as he passed by then followed the female minder to the stern lounge area.

'Mister Shackleton Blister, boss,' said the woman.

Konstantin Mirov and Ivan Permyak stood next to the bar. Two beautiful women sat on a white leather couch drinking champagne. The men were dressed in evening suits.

Mirov nodded to the girl. 'Thank you, Tonya.'

She stepped back.

'Why, Mister Shack. What a nice surprise,' said Mirov. 'To what do we owe the pleasure?'

Shack put his hand in his jacket pocket. Tonya rushed forward, an automatic already aimed at Shack's head. Shack looked at her and gently removed his hand. The girl stepped back. He tossed the two gadgets onto the bar. They clattered along the white-marble counter like a pair of dice on a Vegas craps table.

'These were probably expensive, so I thought you might like 'em back.'

The two men looked at the small camera-bugs. Then looked at each other.

'And there was no need to work-over the old concierge. Real tough guys your boys, beating up an old man.'

Konstantin stepped forward. 'I'm afraid I have no idea what you are talking about, Shack. And these little things,' he picked up one of the bugs, 'are nothing to do with me, my friend.'

The stern look on Shack's face eased, replaced by a slight smile. 'Really? GRU hardware. The best bugs in the world. Nothing to do with you? Yeah right.'

Ivan Permyak held up a bottle of vodka and smiled. 'Let's have drink. We talk. Maybe you come to ballet with us, da? We have great box and is Bolshoi tonight.'

'No thanks mate. Vodka's not really my poison. And as far as the ballet's concerned, the only ones doing any dancing around here are you guys.'

Konni stepped even closer. 'Mister Shack, please. Ivan is right, we should talk.'

'Nah, I don't think so. Just leave Amanda alone, eh? She doesn't have your bloody diary.'

The Russian frowned. 'But we . . .'

Shack raised his hand slightly and shook his head. 'Sorry mate I gotta go . . . So in the words of the great Vinnie Jones, *It's been emotional.*'

As Shack left the two men looked at each other. Then Ivan said, 'Who is Vinnie Jones?'

Chapter Nineteen
'Very Strange'

By Tuesday the weather had taken a turn for the worse. It was in the high twenties but overcast and humid and the forecast was for storms in the south east.

Shack was on the balcony when the first flash of lightning snaked across the sky. A few moments later the thunder rumbled in. He came back inside and looked at his watch. 'He's late.'

Amanda stood and went to the big windows. She slid the patio doors closed then watched the deluge beat down onto the Thames. 'Only a few minutes.'

No sooner had she spoken than the house phone beeped. Shack picked it up. 'Okay thanks. Ask him to come up please.'

A couple of minutes later the doorbell chimed. Shack opened the door.

'Good morning, I'm Detective Constable Peers.'

Shack stepped to one side. 'Mornin, come in.'

Peers offered his hand to Amanda. 'Miss Lang. Good morning.'

They shook hands. 'Hello again. Can I get you a drink? Tea, coffee?'

'No, I'm fine thanks, Miss.'

'This is my friend, Shack.'

Peers nodded and found himself staring at Shack's eye-patch. 'Sir.'

Amanda resumed her seat on the couch and pointed to the chair opposite. 'Please have a seat, Detective.'

He sat down and placed a leather zip-folder on the table. Shack joined Amanda.

The young cop adopted a serious look. 'So, Miss Lang, have you established if there's anything missing?'

She shook her head. 'Doesn't seem to be.'

The cop frowned. 'Really? Nothing stolen, no damage?'

Amanda smiled slightly. 'No. Nothing'

His frown remained. 'Very strange. They beat up the old boy downstairs to get your passcode, yet they take nothing and do no damage.'

Amanda nodded. 'It is, yes. Very strange.'

Shack leaned forward. 'What about CCTV?'

Peers took a tablet from his folder and tapped the screen. A couple of seconds later he passed it across to Shack and Amanda.

They watched in silence as the camera showed the arrival of a van into the basement parking. Three men in black coveralls, baseball caps and gloves, climbed out. All kept their heads low making it obvious they were aware of the CCTV.

The scene flipped to the main entrance and showed the three leaving the lift. At the desk the concierge was punched and manhandled into the rear office. Several minutes later two men came out and got into the elevator.

The scene changed once more. Shack pointed to the seven minute time-lapse at the bottom of the screen as the two men came out of the lift and went into the office. A second or two later all three emerged and took the lift down to the basement.

The final scene showed them getting into the van and driving away.

Shack passed the tablet back to Peers. 'Organised; aware; professional. Not your usual drug-addled burglars.'

The detective frowned. 'Very observant of you, sir. Sounds like you've encountered these types before?'

Shack nodded. 'In the past, yeah.'

'Really? And how would . . .?'

'So what now, detective?' interrupted Amanda.

The cop put the tablet back in his folder, removed a sheet of paper and passed it to her. 'This is the incident report and case number if you need it for your insurance.'

'Which of course I won't as there's nothing to investigate.'

He zipped up the folder and stood up. 'We still have the assault on the concierge. Which we are taking very seriously, Miss. It could have been a lot worse for him.'

'Yes, yes of course. Sorry, I didn't mean . . .'

Peers raised his hand. 'It's okay.' He looked around the stylish apartment. 'Still a mystery though. Why they went to all that trouble to get in here and steal nothing. Don't you think so?'

Amanda frowned slightly. 'Yes, I suppose.'

'Okay. That's all from me, Miss Lang.' He handed her a business card. 'If anything does come up, here's my number.'

'Thank you, Detective Peers.' They shook hands.

Shack offered his hand. 'Yeah, thanks detective.'

The young cop looked Shack in the eye and smiled slightly. 'Good morning, Sir.'

After the detective had gone, Amanda said. 'Well, that was a waste of time.'

Shack went to the big windows and watched the rain bounce on the balcony tiles. He didn't speak for several seconds. 'Maybe not.'

'Oh?'

He turned back to her. 'They get access to the flat and take nothing. They plant the bugs, fair enough. But if they wanted to cover up the reason they broke in they would have stolen something. Right?'

'Yes, I think we established that the other day. Get in and steal something would make it look like a regular burglary. To cover up their real intentions to bug the place.'

'That's right. But by not taking anything they force us to ask the question. Why did they do it?'

'But what if we hadn't found the bugs?'

'True, we might not have done. But then they'd have us under surveillance.'

'But we did find them.'

'And that, Y'Ladyship sends their message.'

'Which is . . . they are not going to leave us alone.'

Shack nodded. 'Pretty much, yeah.'

'And what about your little trip over to the *Angelina* last evening? You went there to wind them up. Didn't you?'

He grinned. 'Partly, yeah. But also to let them know we're onto them.'

'So what now?'

'Now I'm gonna make a nice pot of tea.'

'That's it?'

As he passed her he kissed her cheek. 'Then we are going to spend the rest of the day going through the diary and journal transcripts.'

Chapter Twenty
'God's Holy Trousers'

Victoria Tower Gardens, adjacent to The Palace of Westminster, is no more than a two minute walk from the Parliament building's main entrance.

Each day Sir Rowland Deveraux would take a forty-minute break and read his paper on the last bench in the gardens. The earlier downpour had moved north taking the dark storm clouds with it. A watery sun now sparkled on the surface of the slow moving Thames.

Big Ben chimed one o'clock. He took out a handkerchief and dabbed at the last of the rain drops on the bench. It was almost ten minutes later when another man sat down. Neither acknowledged the other.

Deveraux continued to read the Times. 'You're late, *tovarish.*'

'Yes, I'm sorry. Traffic.'

Sir Rowland turned a page, shook the paper straight and said, 'It would appear things are getting totally out of control, old boy.'

'Yes but we . . .'

'But? But nothing. And please do not give me your excuses. It's distasteful enough having to deal with you people without having to endure your ineptitude.'

'You people? Who the hell do you think you're talking to?'

Another page was turned. Deveraux glanced sideways. 'I know all too well who I'm talking to. And don't think all your money and contacts can intimidate me. You Russians are all the same with your money and mafia.'

'Be careful, Sir Rowland. You really don't want to make an enemy of us.'

'You think I'm afraid of you?' the paper was shaken straight again. 'My ancestors came over with William the Conqueror. My family have been loyal civil servants to the Crown since Cromwell chopped off a king's head. What I do, I do for England. . . . Not money. And certainly not because I'm afraid of you.'

'Yes. But you're still happy to accept our money, aren't you, Sir Rowland? And as for your England . . well . . . we know its darkest secret.'

For several seconds neither man spoke.

Deveraux turned slightly and peered over the top of his spectacles. 'Definitely not one of our more honourable episodes, I must admit. But that was a hundred years ago. Today is what is important.'

'That's right. So why are we meeting?'

'Four people dead, A fifth beaten senseless. Police investigations. Need you ask why?'

'We must gut the sturgeon if we are to extract the caviar.'

Deveraux glanced sideways and sighed deeply. 'But your *sturgeons* have not produced the damned diary, have they?'

'Not yet, no. But we believe we know who has it.'

Again the paper was shaken. 'You believe? And who pray, do you believe has it?'

'A journalist.'

'God's holy trousers! A bloody journalist.'

'She befriended Irina Seranova. They spent quite a lot of time together before the old woman went to Devon. We think she was doing a story on Irina.'

'Oh, this just gets better and better. Why didn't you take the book from the old woman the moment you discovered she had it?'

'She was being protected.'

'Protected?'

'Yes. The Romanovia. She was one of them. They were protecting her.'

'Oh, for God's sake, not another shadowy organisation Do they actually exist? Or are they just another fantasy like the Illuminati?'

For the first time the man turned to Deveraux. He lowered his voice. 'Oh, they exist, Sir Rowland. They are part of the Templari Incrementum and dedicated to returning a true Tsar to the Russian throne.'

Sir Rowland folded his paper and looked out across the Thames. 'If the Templari are involved then you'd better move quickly, old boy.

'So, you know of this organisation?'

'It's a while since I took Latin. But yes, I do . . . The Descendants of the Templars.'

Chapter Twenty One
'Mastermind'

It was almost 7pm when Shack and Amanda finished studying the translations of Irina's mother's diary and father's journal. They'd both made notes and highlighted areas of interest and intrigue. It was clear to them there was far more to these tomes than a potted history of two remarkable people.

'So, partner, now we've gone through them both in detail, what do you think?'

Shack leaned back and stretched his arms above his head. 'Amazin.'

'Amazing for sure.'

He leaned forward and flicked through the pages. Then stopped at one. 'So the Tsar trusted Andrei Volodin with the Romanov treasure. I mean how much is that gonna be worth?'

She nodded. 'Millions back then, probably billions in today's currency.'

'Nicholas obviously knew he was going to be toppled and this was his plan to secure his dynasty.'

'Yes. Get all the treasure out. Stop the Bolsheviks getting their hands on it.'

Shack stood up. 'I'm gonna have a beer. Do you want something?'

'Yes please. I'll have a glass of that Merlot.'

A few moments later Shack returned. He handed her the wine. 'It's after seven.'

She nodded. 'Yes, the day's flown past.'

He swallowed a mouthful of beer then picked up the journal transcript. He read again. 'So, Captain Volodin was only twenty-seven when he left Moscow with the *children* . . . the five code-named trunks.'

Amanda sipped her wine then nodded. 'Yes, and from what it says in there,' she pointed to the journal, 'he made his way to England.'

Shack flipped over more pages. 'And Larisa, his fiancé, joined him a couple of months later.'

'Yes. She was twenty-five and already pregnant.'

Shack turned a couple of pages. 'And according to this, when Volodin found out she was pregnant he insisted they married immediately.'

'As he would, being in love with her.'

'But the child, Irina, was born in October. According to this the Captain left early January.'

Amanda took another sip of wine. 'Yes . . . do the math.'

Shack went to the kitchen, returning with another beer and the bottle of Merlot. He topped up her glass. 'So, are we to believe Volodin was not Irina's father? Or that her mother had an extended pregnancy?'

Amanda picked up the transcript. '*That* is the question.'

Shack frowned. 'I guess all will be revealed in due course. What about dinner, Y'Ladyship?'

'I'd rather not go out and there's not much in the fridge . . . How about Chinese?'

'Okay. The usual?'

'Yes, please.'

Shack made the call.

After they'd eaten they returned to the transcripts. For many minutes they read in silence.

'It's clear from the journal that four of the trunks were brought south,' said Amanda, 'but *Anastasia,* the fifth trunk, is unaccounted for.'

Shack leaned over. 'Let me see.' He read on for a few minutes. 'Yeah, you're right. Only four came south with Captain Volodin.'

'So what happened to *Anastasia*?'

He raised his eye-patch wiped the area underneath with the back of his hand. 'The answer's got to be in here somewhere.'

'Oh, you really should be on Mastermind.'

The hurt look on Shack's face made her laugh. 'Sorry, darling, couldn't resist.'

He continued to read then looked at her. 'Pass me the postcards, please.'

She opened the journal and took out the cards. 'Have you found something?'

He didn't answer. He spread the old sepia cards on the table then returned to the transcript.

'Well? . . . Shack?'

He looked up and smiled then passed her one of the cards. 'Look at this.'

She adjusted her spectacles and studied the image. 'Okay?'

He handed her the transcript and tapped the page. 'Now read that.'

She cleared her throat and read out loud . . . *In ancient halls betrayal walks in hand with greed and fear. Four children taken now will stay and non shall shed a tear. One noble stands alone amidst a storm that has no end. A kingly heart is weak and leaves it's blood alone to fend.* A few moments passed and then. 'Oh, my God, yes.' She looked at the card again. 'Maybe you *should* be on Mastermind.'

Chapter Twenty Two
'Camden Lock'

Sir Rowland Deveraux's home was in Berkshire. The old manor house on the outskirts of Thatcham was gifted to the Deveraux family in the 17th century by Cromwell himself. The ancient pile was Sir Rowland's pride and joy and where he'd lived since his birth, fifty years ago. Handed down to the eldest son, the house would always be the home of the Deveraux.

Over the centuries his family had built up a reputation as *King Makers*. Not for them the transient positions as Back-Benchers, Ministers or even Premiers. They, the Deveraux, were always in the background. The ever constant Civil Servants that oiled the wheels of government. Grey-men in the shadows. Regardless of who was in temporary power they never lost theirs. And for the last twenty years Sir Rowland Deveraux had held the most senior and powerful post of all civil servants, that of Cabinet Secretary.

On Tuesdays, Wednesdays, and Thursdays he chose to stay in town, thus avoiding the hour and a half journey back to Berkshire. A practice both he and his wife Eleonor found advantageous. She didn't have to endure his tedious daily reports on what was happening within government and he was free from time to time to discreetly enjoy his more basic urges. This evening in his stylish Camden Lock pied-à-terre he awaited the arrival of someone who would cater to such desires.

It was almost ten o'clock and following the morning's storm the evening had become somewhat humid. He poured himself a large Cognac and went out onto the balcony. A few locals and tourists milled around Camden Basin but thankfully not as many as on a weekend.

He sat down, swirled the brandy in the balloon then sniffed the heady aroma. 'Mmmm,' he said after taking a sip.

The meeting with the Russian had played on his mind all day. He was angry at their ineptitude yet annoyed at himself for getting so wound up. *Who the hell do they think they are?* he thought. He took another drink then his thoughts brought a slight smile to his face. *The Russians had become allies. Nowadays the new threat came from further east, China, North Korea, Iran. Even the Americans were happy to co-operate with the new capitalist Russian Federation.*

He raised his glass and said out loud. 'The New World Order.'

But then the smile disappeared as he remembered the journalist. *And not just any journalist. Amanda Lang . . . Lady Amanda Lang the very woman who'd exposed his old colleague, Sir Anthony Fairfax, now serving twenty-five years at Her Majesty's Pleasure.*

He swallowed the last of his drink. The doorbell rang and his smile returned as he walked back inside. As he passed the mirror he looked at himself and smiled again, then opened the door.

'Good evening. I'm Carlo.'

Deveraux stood for a second and looked at the handsome young man. 'Do come in, Carlo.'

* * *

Marjorie Buchanan had been Sir Rowland Deveraux's
Senior PA for the last twelve years. In all that time she'd
never known him miss a day's work or be late into the
office. She, and indeed all his staff knew when he stayed
in Camden he was always in by seven-thirty. When he
failed to show-up for the nine o' clock briefing she
called his mobile. No reply. She rang the Camden
apartment. No reply. Reluctantly, for fear of alarming
Lady Eleanor, she called his home in Buckinghamshire.
Deveraux's wife had not seen him since Monday.
Marjorie rang his mobile number three more times. By
10 o'clock she was genuinely concerned. She called the
motor pool and requested a motorcycle courier. Within
minutes a leather clad young woman presented herself at
Marjorie's office.

'What's your name?'

'Jill, ma'am.'

'You know Sir Rowland's Camden Lock address,
Jill?'

The young woman took out her phone and tapped the
screen. A second or two later she smiled. 'Yes, ma'am, I
have it here.'

Marjorie took a key from her drawer and handed it
across. 'This is a spare key. Go and see if Sir Rowland is
there. If he's alright, call me soon as you're in the flat.'

The courier nodded. 'Very good, ma'am.'

Twenty minutes after leaving the Palace of Westminster Jill knocked on Deveraux's door. Nothing. She knocked a little harder. No reply.

She unlocked the door and entered. 'Sir Rowland?' She raised her voice. 'Sir Rowland?'

The courier looked around the smart sitting room. No sign of Deveraux. On the table was a half empty bottle of Cognac and a couple of glasses, a film of white powder and a small plastic bag. Again she called out. Again no reply.

She took out her phone and called Marjorie Buchanan. 'There's no one here, ma'am.'

'You've checked the whole apartment?'

'Er . . . no ma'am. I'm in the lounge.'

'For goodness sake girl, have a look.'

Jill opened a door. The tiny kitchen was empty. She crossed the sitting room and opened the other door. 'Oh God!'

Buchanan's voice came over the phone. 'What is it? Jill? What is it?'

She put the phone to her ear. 'I think they're dead.'

'What?'

The courier looked at the two naked men. Deveraux was slumped across the bed. She couldn't see his face. A young man was on the floor, eyes wide open, dried blood in his nostrils.

'Jill? Jill?'

'I'm here.'

'You sure he's dead. Have you checked?'

'Er . . . no ma'am.'

'For God sake girl check his pulse or something.'

Jill moved slowly towards the motionless figure. She touched his shoulder. 'He's warm.'

'What?'

'Sir Rowland . . . he feels warm.'

Chapter Twenty Three
'Lucky and Leach'

It took over two hours for Lady Eleanor to get from Thatcham to Saint Thomas's. On the south end of Westminster Bridge the hospital stands directly opposite the Houses of Parliament. As she stepped out of her car she looked across the river at her husband's place of work.

'Bloody place!' she said under her breath.

She quickly made her way to Intensive Care. As she approached Reception she saw Giles her youngest son, with Marjorie Buchanan. The boy stood up and rushed to her. 'Mum.'

'It's alright, darling. He's going to be fine. Are you okay?'

'Yes, yes, I'm good. I was just so worried in case I didn't get here in time. One of the chaps from college gave me a lift on his motorbike.'

'In time? Don't be silly, darling. He's not going to die.'

'But, mum . . .'

She kissed his cheek. 'Shush now. Pull yourself together and sit down while I talk to a doctor.'

He looked at his watch. 'It's nearly nine o'clock in Washington. Have you called, Andrew?'

'Yes. Your brother was going into a meeting with the Ambassador. He'll call back later. Now please sit down and let me find out what's happened to your father.' She turned to Buchannan. 'Thank you for being here, Marjorie. Would you stay with Giles please?'

The doctor offered his hand. 'Doctor Shah.'

As they shook she said. 'Eleonor Deveraux. How is my husband doctor?'

'Sir Rowland is in a coma but stable.'

'What on earth happened?'

Shah stepped to one side and lowered his voice. 'We believe the cocaine he took was laced with ricin.'

For several seconds she looked at the doctor, unable to speak. 'Cocaine! Ricin?'

'Yes. He's incredibly lucky to be alive.'

'Lucky? He's in a coma.'

The doctor frowned. 'Well . . . luckier than the other man, Lady Eleanor.'

She took in a deep breath. 'Other man?'

'Yes. A boy of about twenty I'm told. He's downstairs in the morgue.'

* * *

As Lady Eleanor waited to see her husband; in Devon the inquiry into Julie Lawson's death was about to begin.

Meeting Room 4 in the Torbay Coroner's Office was full. Over twenty people sat in the public section with six more upfront in the witness area.

The clerk stood as the Coroner entered. 'Quiet please.'

The inquiry had been underway for almost an hour when the final witness took the stand.

The clerk handed him a small Bible and card. 'Please state your full name and read from this.'

'Mickey . . . oh sorry. Michael Robert Leach.'

As he recited the oath his broad Devon accent brought a smattering of laughter from several present.

'Quiet please,' snapped the clerk.

Unfazed, Mickey took his seat.

The coroner sipped from a glass of water. 'Mister Leach. Please tell us what you saw on the morning in question.'

'Aye, judge.' Again sniggers from the audience.

The coroner looked over his spectacles. 'If I have any more of that I shall clear the room.'

He turned back to Mickey and smiled. 'I'm not a judge Mister Leach but you may if you wish address me as sir. Now please go on.'

Leach smiled. 'Aye, judge . . . Sur. Well I were out in m'normal place. An I sor the yung lady.'

'Your usual place?'

'Aye, sur. Near t'old tower. I likes it best there.'

'You mean the derelict watch tower on Steeple Point?'

Mickey nodded. 'Aye sur that's it.'

'But the tower must be some distance from the incident scene, Mister Leach.'

Leach put his head to one side as if in deep though. 'Er . . . Half mile mebee. Aye sur. Bout half mile.'

'That's quite a distance. And yet you say you saw what happened.'

Mickey frowned. 'Aye sur. Clear as a bell. I ad me nokks.'

'I'm sorry. Nokks?'

'Binok'ylas.'

'Ah . . . binoculars.'

Mickey put his shoulders back and in a proud voice declared. 'Aye sur. A'm a twitchur.'

The audience broke into laughter.

The coroner stood up and glared. The room fell silent.

'Last warning.' He resumed his seat. 'Please go on, Mister Leach. So you were birdwatching.'

'Aye. A saw urr cummin tords me. Bout half mile away. Then saw t'other two from bushes.'

'Bushes?'

'Aye. A large patch o' bushes wi some nestin swallers. We only get em down here in . . .'

'Mister Leach. Please. The two men?'

'Oh right . . . aye. Well y'see sur it was all s'quick. They just rushed at poor lass. Picked urr up kinda thing. Then dropped urr ovr cliff.'

'And you saw this clearly Mister Leach?'

'Oh aye, sur. Clear as church bell.'

'Were you able to get a good look at the assailants?'

'Sorry, sur?'

'Her attackers, Mister Leach.'

'Oh right. Not really sur. Both ad elmets.'

'Elmets?'

Mickey put his hands on his head. 'Aye sur. Moturbike elmets.'

Chapter Twenty Four
'Not This One'

In Hammersmith, Shack and Amanda were waiting for the Uber. It was a little after one when her phone beeped. 'Taxi is here.'

'Okay.' Shack came out of his bedroom. 'Got everything?'

She nodded. 'Let's go.'

Twenty minutes later the cab pulled-up in Parliament Square a few yards from Churchill's imposing statue.

'This okay for you guys?' said the driver.

Amanda smiled and tapped her credit card on the screen. 'Fine. Thank you.'

They stepped out and headed towards the Parliament building. As they passed Winston, Shack looked up and smiled.

Amanda caught sight of the gesture and linked her arm through his. 'One of your heroes?'

'Sure is.'

They crossed the busy road then through the gate into Black Rod's Garden.

The friendly police officer nodded. 'Good afternoon.'

'Parliamentary Archive,' said Amanda.

'Yes, Miss. Straight ahead to Security. Then you'll need to complete registration.'

She smiled. 'Thank you officer. I've visited the Archive before.'

'Very good, Miss. You'll know the procedure then.'

Inside they joined the small queue waiting to go through the airport-style security. The only difference was this area was monitored by heavily-armed police.

'You've been here before then?'

She nodded. 'A couple of times doing research.'

They used the trays for their personal effects and passed through the body scanner. On the other side they went to the reception desk. ID's were presented and the lady behind the counter punched their names into the computer.

She handed Amanda a VISTOR badge. 'That's fine, Miss.' Then gave Shack a card. 'You'll need to complete a registration please, sir.'

He nodded and stepped to the side. A few minutes later he returned the card. Again the receptionist tapped at her keyboard. 'That's fine sir.'

With their VISITOR badges clipped on they followed the signs to the Archive main office.

A jolly-faced lady greeted them. 'How can we help you today?'

Amanda had prepared a list of documents. 'These are what we would like to see please.'

The lady put on her spectacles and studied the paper. With a pen she moved down the list. 'Hmm. Hmm. Alright. Yes. Hmm. Oh . . . Oh not this one.' She turned the paper back to Amanda and pointed to the last item. 'This won't be available today I'm afraid.'

Amanda looked at the sheet then back to the lady. 'I thought this was in the public domain now?'

Shack leaned forward. 'Excuse me.' the woman looked at the one-eyed man. This time Shack smiled. He pointed to the item. 'We understood this was sealed for a hundred years in 1917. So the restriction must have ended two years ago?'

She removed her spectacles. 'Just a second please.' Again she tapped on her keyboard, reading the screen as she did so. She looked up. 'The documents you have requested are available but not the last one . . . Not today.'

'Ah,' said Amanda, 'sorry we were confused for a second. You mean we can get access but not today?'

The lady smiled and nodded. 'That's correct.'

'So when would it be available?'

The lady frowned. 'I'm not sure, Miss. That particular document requires special permission to be released.'

'And how do we get that?' said Shack.

'A dispensation from the Cabinet Secretary's Office.' She tapped her screen. 'Actually the Cabinet Secretary needs to sign off on it.'

'Okay. So when can we see him?'

'I really can't say. I'm not sure when Sir Rowland will be back.'

'Sir Rowland?' said Amanda.

'Yes . . . Sir Rowland Deveraux, the Cabinet Secretary.'

Amanda saw the frustration on Shack's face as he said, 'What? Is he on holiday or something? Is there no deputy? What?'

The lady leaned back in her chair. 'I believe he was rushed into hospital this morning. And yes there is a deputy, but he doesn't have the authorisation with regards to this item . . . I'm sorry, sir.'

'Okay thank you,' said Amanda. 'we'd still like to go through the other items if we may please.'

The jolly-lady's smile returned. 'Certainly, miss.'

As they entered the Archive office Shack leaned close to Amanda and said quietly, 'Now what the hell is so sensitive it needs the Cabinet Secretary's authorisation?'

Three hours later the bell advising the Archive was closing rang. Shack looked at his watch. 'Four o'clock already.'

Amanda leaned back from the screen and rubbed the back of her neck. 'Okay. Time to go.' She collected the papers and notes together and slipped them into the zip-folder. 'That was interesting.'

'Yeah . . . and certainly informative, Y'Ladyship.'

As they passed the desk they nodded to the jolly lady and said, 'Thank you.'

She smiled at Amanda. Shack got a slight scowl.

Outside the street was wet from a fine evening drizzle. Nevertheless it was pleasantly warm and far more comfortable than the chilled atmosphere of the air-conditioned Archive. Over on Parliament Square Lawns a man quickly rose from a bench. As Amanda and Shack exited the gate he swiftly tapped out a WhatsApp message. *They are leaving the archive now.*

Chapter Twenty Five
'Local News'

At that time of day it took a while to find a cab but they still managed to get back to Hammersmith before 5 o'clock.

'I need a shower and a couple of Paracetamol,' said Amanda.

Shack frowned. 'You okay, Y'Ladyship?'

'No not really. I've an awful headache after the Archive'

'Why don't you go have a nap, luv?'

It was almost six when Amanda returned. There was still a light drizzle but Shack had opened the patio doors to get some air. A cafetiere was on the table. He was watching the news as she came in, a bottle of Stella in his hand. 'Feel better?'

She let out a sigh as she sank into the big armchair. 'Much. And you made fresh coffee.'

He smiled. 'Heard your shower going.' He poured the coffee then passed her the mug.

She smiled as she took the first mouthful. 'Oh, that's lovely.'

They sat in silence for several minutes and watched the national news. Then at six-thirty the local news began. Shack got up and went for another beer.

As he came back in Amanda said, 'Look at this.'

One half of the screen showed a reporter in front of a large sign, ACCIDENT & EMERGENCY. Across the bottom of the screen the caption read, LIVE FROM ST THOMAS'S HOSPITAL. The other half of the screen showed a photo of a very smart middle aged gentlemen in a three piece suit. The caption below read, SIR ROWLAND DEVERAUX. CABINET SECRETARY.

Amanda and Shack watched as the young man spoke. *'Yes Tom, the doctors have advised Sir Rowland is still in a coma but stable. A young man, as yet unnamed, was found dead at Sir Rowland's flat in Camden Lock. We've been told the cocaine they'd taken was possibly laced with ricin, although as yet this is unconfirmed. At the moment the police are looking into the incident and of course are keen to interview Sir Rowland as soon as possible. Now back to you in the studio.'*

Shack swallowed a mouthfull of beer then nodded to the TV. 'So that's Sir Rowland Deveraux. The joker who's supposed to allow us access to the Archive.'

Amanda nodded. 'The very same, darling.'

Shack finished the bottle. 'Bit of a coincidence don't you think?'

'Perhaps. But then again . . . who knows?'

Not far away in Kensington, Count Oleg Stranski stood up and went to the window. He too had just seen the Deveraux report. For several seconds he looked out over his lush garden. The rain had made mirror-like puddles on the big patio. He turned to the other man in the room and frowned. 'Send Lady Deveraux some flowers with our best wishes, Alexi.'

Onboard *Angelina,* Konstantin Mirov and Ivan Permyak had also watched the London news. Ivan went to the bar and poured another vodka. He swallowed it in one, turned to Konni and grinned. 'Cocainum and queers eh? These so-called English aristocrats have no honour.'

Konstantin joined him at the bar. He picked up the bottle and filled their glasses. 'You are right, brother. No honour at all. Cocainum and queers . . . is a dangerous mix I think.'

Ivan winked. 'And with a little ricin, is much more dangerous.'

They raised their glasses and laughed. 'Nostrovia.'

Chapter Twenty Six
'Carlton Lambert'

At breakfast and with the possibility of not getting back into the Archive any time soon, Shack had suggested they return to Irina's solicitors.

Amanda wasn't so sure. 'I can't see how they are likely to tell us anything, darling. You know what these people are like. It's all confidential this and confidential that.'

Shack put down the bacon sandwich and wiped his mouth. 'They've just had one of the partners murdered. I think that might galvanise them into being a little more . . . open.'

Amanda finished her coffee then stood up. 'Okay, you could be right . . . I'll make the call.'

Carlton Lambert was the typical high powered senior partner. Suits and shirts from Saville Row and Jermyn Street, shoes from Lobb. Shack looked at the chain across the front of the stylish waistcoat. The discreet Square & Compass hanging from the gold Albert brought a slight smile. As they shook hands Shack covered the grip with his left hand and looked into Lambert's eyes.

The Masonic handshake between the men did not go un-noticed by Amanda.

Lambert turned to her 'Please have a seat, Miss Lang. Can we get you anything to drink?'

She smiled and shook her head. 'Thank you for seeing us at short notice, Mister Lambert.'

The solicitor made a slight dismissive gesture, then took his seat behind the big desk. 'So, how may we help you today?'

'First let me offer our condolences. What happened to Miss Arnold was dreadful.'

'Yes indeed. We are all still in shock. Awful. Awful.'

A few reflective moments passed then Amanda continued. 'We were hoping you may be able to help us with something we are looking into.'

Lambert frowned. 'Looking into?'

'Yes. I had become friends with one of your clients. Irina Seranova.'

'Ah yes, Irina. A long standing and respected client. Also sadly departed.'

'You know, I think I will have some water please?'

Lambert touched a small screen on the desk. 'Lucy could we have some water please?' He looked back to Amanda. 'Please go on, Miss Lang.'

'So, our question is. Can you tell us anything more about Irina Seranova?'

Lucy arrived carrying a tray with small bottles of water and tumblers.

Lambert smiled. 'Just leave it there, Lucy. We'll manage, thank you.'

'Yes, sir.'

Amanda opened a bottle and poured some into a glass. She swallowed a mouthful, then said, 'So . . . might that be possible, Mister Lambert?'

He cleared his throat then leaned forward, hands on the desk. 'As I'm sure you know, Miss Lang we have a duty of confidentiality to . . .'

'Excuse me, sir,' interrupted Shack. 'Irina Seranova's death is still under investigation. A young woman who was caring for Irina has been murdered. Your colleague, Miss Arnold and her husband have been killed and we believe they may not be the last. We really need your help, sir. So, with respect, please can you help us?'

Lambert sat back and looked at the one-eye man. Several seconds passed then he removed his spectacles and ran his fingers across his forehead.

'Mister Lambert . . . please. This is very important,' said Amanda.

The solicitor picked up a bottle of water and poured a glass. 'Yes, Yes. I understand.'

'Will you help us, sir?' said Shack.

Lambert took a drink then wiped his lips with a handkerchief. He stood up, went to the window and looked down onto Chancery Lane. The road was full of traffic. He watched a cyclist weave in and out between the vehicles.

Shack got up. 'Mister Lambert, please?'

The dapper gent turned and nodded. 'Very well.' He returned to his desk. 'Irina Seranova was a client for many years. We handled all her requirements since my father was senior partner. Indeed he brought Irina to the practice.'

Amanda nodded. 'What about her estate?'

'Yes. Yes we are of course her executors.'

'And who are the beneficiaries?' said Shack.

Lambert took another mouthful of water. 'We administer Irina's . . . the Seranova trust fund. From there we make a payment on the twenty-third of February each year.'

'An annual payment?' said Amanda.

'Yes . . . One-hundred thousand pounds. Every year for the last forty years.'

'Wow,' said Shack. 'And that money went to Irina?'

Lambert shook his head. 'No. The payment is transferred to a small private bank in the city.'

'Is?' said Shack.

'Sorry? said the solicitor.

'You said is. Not was.'

'Ah . . . yes. The payment will continue.'

Amanda looked at Shack, then back to Lambert. 'So if the money wasn't going to Irina and will continue to be made. Who's the beneficiary?'

Lambert took a deep breath and looked at Amanda. 'Her name is Anna Seranova.'

Chapter Twenty Seven
'East Lodge'

Luton Hoo Golf Hotel & Spa is probably the best five star establishment in Bedfordshire. The building as it stands today was redesigned by Thomas Adam. The extensive gardens and surrounding parkland are the work of Capability Brown. The main house and estate had, over the years, been owned by various members of the aristocracy. One of whom was Sir Julius Wernher who purchased the property at the turn of the twentieth century. In 1917 Wernher's second son Harold married Countess Mikhailovna Torby, a senior member of the Romanov dynasty. From that day forward, and until the early nineties, the estate had always maintained close links with the Romanovs.

Amanda stopped at the front of the imposing hotel. Shack lowered his window as a liveried doorman approached. 'Good afternoon, sir. Checking in?'

Shack smiled as he looked up at the huge portico columns. 'Sadly not today. We're looking for *East Lodge.*'

'Ah, very good sir.' He removed his bowler-hat and leaned in a little closer to address Amanda. 'Go back to the main drive, madam. Turn right towards the golf house. Follow the drive around until you come to a fork. The golf house is to the left, *East Lodge* to the right. Just follow that road down the hill to the far side of the estate.'

Amanda nodded. 'Thank you.'

He stepped back, put his hat on and touched the brim. 'You're welcome, madam.'

As they pulled away from the front of the magnificent building, Shack saw a tear run down Amanda's cheek. 'You okay?'

She sniffed and brushed the tear with the back of her hand. 'Just being silly.'

'What is it, Amanda?'

She smiled at him. He never called her Amanda. She saw the concern in his eye. 'I've been here before. Just brought back memories.'

'Yeah?'

'Samantha and I came here for our anniversary.'

Shack smiled. 'Well that's nice . . . isn't it?'

'The week before she was killed.'

'Oh, God . . . I'm so sorry.'

She sniffed again. 'I'm fine, darling. Really I'm fine. Just being silly.'

They turned right past the eyesore that is the contemporary golf house, down the hill and through the small wood. About a quarter of a mile further on they saw two buildings, one each side of a large ornate gate.

'That must be the east entrance,' said Shack, 'looks like it's been closed for years.'

'Yes. The main entrance is the one we came through on the west side of the estate.'

Each single storey building was obviously occupied, with mature gardens to the front and cars parked at the side. A thin wisp of white smoke floated up from one of the chimneys.

'They were the old gatekeepers' cottages,' said Amanda.

'Someone's got themselves a lovely place to live now then.'

As they passed a huge larch they saw a discreet sign, EAST LODGE. They turned off the road and onto a short drive.

'Oh yes,' said Shack, 'very nice.'

East Lodge was about a hundred yards from the road, with manicured gardens to the front and several mature trees to the rear. The two storey structure was in total keeping with the elegant estate and although not huge wouldn't have been out of place on *The Real Housewives of Cheshire.*

They stopped in front and climbed out. 'This is class,' said Shack.

He smiled at the knocker on the studded oak door. Instead of the usual lion's face, an ornately gilded double-headed eagle sparkled in the afternoon sun. The unmistakable symbol of the Romanov's.

Amanda tapped out a rhythmic knock and waited. No reply. Again she knocked, this time with greater force. The banging on the door disturbed a pair of blackbirds who took off in a flutter of wings and tweets.

Several moments passed without answer. 'Let's check around back,' said Shack.

The rear gardens were even more beautiful than the front. As they knocked on the back door an old man appeared from behind one of the huge hydrangeas. 'Hello?'

They turned. 'Oh, hello,' said Amanda.

The man smiled and removed his hat. 'Can I help you, young lady?'

'Yes, please. We're here to see Miss Seranova.'

He came forward, the limp in his left leg clearly noticeable. 'She's not here.'

'Any idea when she'll be back, sir?'

The man smiled at the respectful *sir*. 'Not really sure. She hasn't been home since last Saturday.'

'Oh,' said Amanda, 'she on holiday or something?'

The old boy frowned. 'I'm not really sure.'

'But you said she hasn't been here since Saturday.'

'That's right.'

'You saw her leave?' said Shack.

'I was in my garden. I live in one of the old gatehouses.'

Shack smiled and made a sweeping gesture with his hand. 'Oh nice, great place to live.'

'Yes. Been here for almost twenty years.' He tapped his leg. 'Ever since I lost this in the army.' He pointed to Shack's eye-patch. 'Looks like you've been in the wars as well, young fella?'

Shack touched the patch. 'Nothing so noble, sir.'

Amanda stepped forward. 'You said you saw her leave?'

'Yes. In the morning. Strange thing is, she usually lets me know if she's going to be away. I look after her garden and generally keep an eye on her.'

'So she drove off without telling you?'

'Yes . . . well no not really. I saw her go. She left in a Range Rover . . . looked to be a couple of other chaps in there as well.'

'Someone came for her then?'

'That's what it looked like. As I said, she never mentioned it to me. All very sudden.'

Amanda smiled. 'Okay. Well thank you for your time, sir.'

'No problem at all. Any message for when she does get back?' He gave a little smile. 'She's never been so popular.'

'Oh, really?' said Shack.

'Yes. Someone else showed up looking for her on Saturday afternoon, In a beautiful old Bentley.'

Chapter Twenty Eight
'Hammersmith Bridge'

It was early evening by the time they got back to Amanda's flat. They parked, then took the elevator to the foyer. As they stepped out to change lifts, George the concierge appeared from the back office.

Amanda said, 'Hold it a second, darling.' She went over to the desk. 'Hello, George. How are you feeling?'

There was still some bruising around his eye which made him flinch as he smiled. 'Good evening, Miss Lang. I'm fine, Miss. Thank you for asking.'

She returned the smile. 'Okay, good. You take care now, George.'

A few moments later they entered the apartment. The tiny blue light on the phone blinked.

'Voice mail.'

'What?'

She picked up the handset and said again, 'Voice mail.'

He watched as she listened to the playback. She tapped the phone again and the speaker filled the room. *Anna Seranova will be in the middle of Hammersmith Bridge this evening at nine o'clock.*

They looked at each other for several seconds, then Shack spoke, 'Now what the hell is that all about?'

Amanda checked her watch, seven-fifteen. She pointed to the phone. 'And who the hell was that?'

'There's some weird shit going on here, Y'Ladyship.'

She rubbed the back of her neck. 'I couldn't have put it better myself.'

Shack grinned. 'Well perhaps more politely . . . So what d'you think?'

'I'm going to shower, then have something to eat.'

He frowned. 'That's it?'

She kissed his cheek and headed to her room. 'Then, darling, we are going for a little stroll.'

Due to recent cracks in the structure, Hammersmith Bridge had been closed to heavy vehicles since April. Now only bicycles and motor bikes were allowed and the bridge had effectively become a pedestrian facility.

It only took them a few minutes to walk from Amanda's apartment to the bridge. By eight fifty-five it was almost dark and the illuminations that festooned the iconic landmark twinkled in the dying light of the day. Lycra-clad cyclists and the odd motor scooter were the only traffic using the crossing. Both pavements were quite busy with walkers, joggers, and groups of tourists.

They arrived in the centre of the bridge a couple of minutes before nine. They had no idea what the woman looked like and there was no one waiting at the location. On the other side of the road a small cluster of Japanese were heading to the south bank. As they passed the centre of the bridge Amanda saw the woman. She squeezed Shack's arm. 'Across the road.'

The woman looked to be in her thirties, smartly dressed with a large handbag hanging from her shoulder. They waited for a group of chattering cyclists to pass, then quickly crossed the road. The woman appeared nervous, looking up and down the bridge as Shack and Amanda approached.

Amanda smiled. 'Anna?'

'Yes . . . You are Amanda Lang?' The accent was clearly Russian.

'Yes, and this is my friend Shack.'

The woman was becoming more nervous by the second.

Shack smiled. 'We're friends. We don't want to harm you.'

'We'd like to talk to you about Irina Seranova,' said Amanda.

The woman said nothing. Her hand was in the bag. She glanced up and down the bridge, then suddenly pulled out a silenced automatic. Shack instinctively stepped in front of Amanda as two gunshots rang out. For a second he was stunned at the noise and the lack of pain. The woman fell back against the handrail, a crimson stain spread across her blouse. A third shot, rang out . . . a small black hole appeared above her right eye as she toppled over the edge.

They rushed to the rail in time to hear the awful shattering of glass, as the body smashed through the riverboat's canopy. The screams of the onboard party-goers echoed under the bridge but were soon drowned out by the screeching of tyres as a powerful motorcycle sped away.

The panic on the party-boat subsided . . . as did the screams. The awful sight of the woman's body now became a subject of curiosity with several of the inebriated revellers filming the macabre scene on their phones.

Shack watched as the helmsman eased the vessel up to a small dock fifty yards west of the bridge. Amanda had already called 999 and sirens could be heard in the distance. A crowd of rubberneckers lined the edge eager to take in the scene below.

Within minutes the first responders arrived . . . a large black van full of heavily armed tactical officers. Two patrol cars, blue lights flashing, entered from the north side and swiftly blocked the access. Another police car took up position on the south side.

Amanda stepped into the road and waved her arms at the heavy mob. An officer ran to her, the rest of his team shouting at the crowd to get off the bridge . . .

It was eleven-fifty when Shack looked at his watch. They'd been in Hammersmith Police Station for almost three hours. He and Amanda had recorded and signed statement transcripts. Several other witnesses had been brought in and were being interviewed, many of whom hardly spoke English.

Out in the foyer, Detective Chief Inspector Reynolds shook hands with Shack. 'Thanks for all your help. There's a car outside; they'll take you home.'

Shack smiled. 'Thank you, sir.'

'But we'd like to talk to you again in the morning, please.'

'No problem.'

Reynolds shook hands with Amanda. 'Thank you, Miss Lang. Try and get some sleep.'

She nodded. 'Thank you, Chief Inspector.'

As they turned to leave Detective Constable Peers came in. 'Miss Lang!'

'Hello again, Detective.'

The young copper looked at her for several seconds, then turned to Shack. 'Everything okay, sir?'

'Yes fine. We're both fine. Thank you.'

'Good night,' said Amanda.

As they left, DCI Reynolds said, 'You know them?'

'Yes, sir. I responded to a break-in at her flat a few nights ago.'

Reynolds looked at his subordinate. 'And?'

'Bit strange really, sir. Nothing taken and no damage. Three heavies knocked the concierge about a bit and got the access code for the flat. But as I said, nothing taken.'

The Chief Inspector looked at the entrance doors. 'And tonight they were involved in the bridge shooting . . . Now is that coincidence, or is there more going on here than they're letting on ?'

'Like I said, sir. Strange.'

Chapter Twenty Nine
'Thank You'

It was a quarter after midnight when the squad car dropped them off at the front of Amanda's building. They hadn't spoken since they left the police station.

They entered the foyer and were greeted by Simon, another of the concierge team. 'Good morning, Miss Lang.'

Amanda acknowledge the pleasantry. 'Morning.'

Shack nodded to Simon, then pressed the lift button. A few moments later they entered the flat. He locked the door and turned around. He was about to speak when she threw her arms around his neck. He felt her shaking.

'You okay, Amanda?'

She never spoke, just held on tightly.

He hugged her close. 'Hey . . . come on, Y'Ladyship, we're okay now.'

She took a deep breath and stepped back. 'Thank you.'

He smiled. 'Thank you?'

'You stepped in front of the gun. You could've been killed. You protected me.'

The shaking continued. A tear trickled down her cheek. *Delayed shock*, he thought; then put his arm around her shoulders. 'Yeah, well it's over now, so sit down. I'll make you a nice cuppa tea.'

'I don't want to sit . . . I'll come with you.' She followed him into the kitchen.

Shack put the kettle on then took a bottle of Hennessey from the cupboard. 'I'd give you a shot of this, but I think hot sweet tea is what you need right now.'

He poured himself a large one as the kettle began to whistle.

She took another glass from the shelf. 'I'll have a brandy as well.'

'You sure? I think you might have a bit of delayed shock.'

She frowned. 'I'm fine. I'll have the tea . . . and a small one of those.'

He passed her the mug, then poured her a shot. He raised his glass. 'Slainte.'

Amanda caught her breath as the fiery liquid slipped down her throat. 'Oh, that's awful.'

'Isn't it just?' Shack picked up the bottle and grinned. 'Now drink your tea, luv . . . you'll feel better.'

'Come on, let's relax a bit before bed. It's been some night.'

In the drawing room they sat for a few minutes. Amanda sipped her tea. Shack poured another large brandy.

She looked at him. For the first time since they left the flat she smiled.

'What?'

Amanda shook her head slightly. 'You stepped in front of that woman's gun.'

He grinned and raised his glass. 'What can I say . . . I laugh at danger.'

'Hmm, yes, I'm sure.'

'So are you feeling any better, darlin?'

'Yes, I think so.' She finished the tea then pointed to the bottle. 'Think I'll have another of those.'

'Really . . . you sure?'

She nodded.

He got a glass from the kitchen and poured her a large one. She looked at the measure and frowned. 'You trying to get me drunk, mister?'

'Help you sleep, luv . . . Cheers.'

Again they sat and drank in silence.

Amanda spoke first. 'So what do you think?'

'About what?'

She frowned. 'Don't be so obtuse. About tonight you fool.'

'Oh, that . . . right.'

'Yes that. So what do you think?'

He finished his drink and poured another. 'You want a top up?'

She held her glass out. 'Please.'

As he poured he said, 'Well I don't think that was Anna, that's for sure.'

Amanda nodded. 'She was definitely Russian though.'

He sat back and swirled his brandy. 'There's a few scenarios here.'

'Which are?'

'She pulls out her gun and was gonna shoot us.'

'Or?'

'She took out the gun to protect us from whoever shot her.'

Amanda shook her head. 'I don't think that's likely. Her look. The way she behaved. We were definitely her target.'

114

Shack nodded. 'Okay, agreed. But then someone shot her first.'

'The motorcyclist.'

He nodded again. 'Yeah. But why was he . . . or she, there?'

'To kill the woman or to kill us?'

Shack swallowed his drink then poured another. 'If the biker was there to kill us, why didn't he? He could've easily taken all three of us out.'

She finished her drink then held out the glass for another. 'Exactly. So if he wasn't there to kill us . . .'

'He was there to take her out!'

Chapter Thirty
'All This Carnage'

Amanda was in the kitchen when Shack entered. She smiled and said, 'Good morning.'

He slumped onto the high-stool and groaned. 'Mornin.' He rubbed his eye. 'You can certainly put it away when you want to, Y'Ladyship.'

'Oh I can rock n' roll with the best of them if the mood takes me, darling.'

'And you look terrific . . . No hangover?'

She smiled. 'Why thank you kind sir.' She poured him some tea. 'And no, I never get hangovers.'

'Lucky you.'

'You want any breakfast?'

He mumbled something and continued sipping his tea. 'I think it was after two when we finished?'

She picked up her mug then kissed his cheek 'Well after two.' She used the remote and switched on the wall TV. 'News!'

The nine o'clock news was just finishing. Shack continued to sip his tea. 'Can you turn that down a little, please?'

She shook her head and lowered the volume. The local London bulletin came on. The newscaster made a few comments, then the image switched to Hammersmith Bridge.

The young reporter began speaking. '*Yes, Tom. Once again the city is shocked as a woman is mercilessly gunned down on Hammersmith Bridge. It was around nine pm last night when the incident occurred. Several witnesses are helping police with their enquiries. The victim's name has not yet been divulged, but we believe she is a foreign national. Yet again we ask . . . just what is the Mayor doing to stop these horrendous acts on our city streets. Now back to you Tom in the studio'.*

Shack groaned. 'Oh, please, luv . . . switch that off.'

She put her arm round his shoulders. 'Come on. Balcony. Fresh air will do you good.'

He groaned again.

* * *

They'd only been waiting a few minutes when DCI Reynolds appeared. 'Good morning. Thanks for coming in again.'

'No problem,' said Shack.

Reynolds waved his hand. 'We're just along here.'

As they entered the interview room Detective Constable Peers stood up. 'Good morning.'

Amanda nodded. 'Morning.'

Shack just nodded.

Reynolds pointed to the chairs on the other side of the table. 'Please . . . have a seat. Can I get you anything before we start? Coffee, water?'

They both shook their heads.

'Right . . . again thank you for coming in. We're going to expand on your statements from last night if that's okay?'

Again they nodded. 'Fine,' said Amanda.

Peers switched on the recorder and spoke. 'Subsequent interview, Hammersmith. Alpha-dash three-three seven, fourteen five nineteen. Present Miss Amanda Lang,

Mister Shackleton Blister, DCI Reynolds, DC Peers. Commence eleven-forty hours.'

Reynolds leaned forward hands clasped on the table. 'The statements you both made last night are pretty much word for word. You both seem to have recalled events in exactly the same way.'

Amanda frowned. 'We were both there, Chief Inspector. Why wouldn't they be similar?'

'Yes of course, but it's usual for multiple witnesses to recall different elements of the same event.'

Shack leaned forward. 'Do we need a brief here?'

Reynolds smiled. 'This is only an interview, sir. You're not under caution. But if you feel you need your solicitor, by all means we can defer the interview.'

Amanda sensed the tension between the two men and put her hand on Shack's arm. 'It's fine. We'll answer your questions.'

The Chief Inspector smiled again. 'Thank you, Miss Lang. So if we . . .'

Amanda interrupted. 'I'm a journalist, DCI Reynolds. I report what I see. Shack here is a Private Investigator, ex detective of your Met. He reports exactly what he sees. It would be fair to say that in our professional capacities we know and understand the importance of recalling events in a salient and un-embellished manner. So I'm sure you will agree that when two such witnesses are involved in the same incident the likelihood of conflicting statements would be rare. In fact it would be more cause for concern if they were conflicting . . . Don't you think, Chief Inspector?'

Reynolds looked at Amanda. Shack lowered his head and smiled. DC Peers turned his head away and smiled.

'Er, okay, Miss Lang . . . Let's move on shall we?'

Amanda held the detective's gaze. 'Yes, let's do that.'

'Last Sunday, DC Peers here was called to an incident at your building in Hammersmith. The concierge was beaten by three intruders and access was gained to your apartment. DC Peers reported that nothing seemed to be taken and no damage appeared to be done. His subsequent interview with you confirmed this.'

'That's correct.'

'Don't you think that strange, Miss Lang?'

'I do. Very strange.'

Reynolds said nothing for several seconds, then turned to Shack. 'What about you, sir?'

'What?'

'That there was nothing taken and no damage. Don't you think that unusual?'

'Who knows what some of these villains are thinking. Maybe they got the wrong flat. Maybe they are just stupid. Who knows? But what's that got to do with last night's shooting?'

Reynolds leaned back then opened the folder in front of him. He looked at the document then raised his head. 'Miss Maxine Arnold. You had a meeting with her last Friday.'

Amanda nodded. 'That's correct.'

'Can you tell us the purpose of that meeting?'

'It was confidential, Chief Inspector, and has nothing to do with last night's shooting.'

'Maxine Arnold and her husband were killed, Miss Lang. You were one of the last clients to meet with her before her death. We could site you with obstruction if . . .'

119

'I was there at Miss Arnold's request. I'd been left something from an old friend, a client of Arnold and Lambert.'

'Might I ask what that was?'

Amanda sighed. 'A Versace scarf.'

'A scarf?'

'Yes.'

'That's it? A scarf?'

'Yes.'

'And the name of this generous benefactor?'

Amanda ignored the sarcastic tone. 'Irina Seranova.'

'And you knew this lady how?'

'I was writing her memoir.'

'Was?'

'Yes, was. Obviously she's dead if I was at her solicitors as a beneficiary.'

'Right, yes of course. And when did she die?'

'A couple of weeks ago. She'd moved to a residential home in Devon.'

'Name of the home please?'

'*Seaview Downs* in Torquay. But I still don't see what all this has to do with last night's shooting.'

Reynolds closed the folder and scratched the back of his neck. 'There's a bit of a pattern here, don't you think, Miss Lang?'

'I'm sorry, Chief Inspector . . . Pattern?'

The detective took a deep breath then leaned back in his chair. 'Maxine Arnold and her husband, dead. Your friend Irina Seranova, dead. The woman you had arranged to meet on the bridge, shot dead. Your concierge beaten and your flat broken into. All this carnage seems to be following you around, Miss Lang.'

Shack stood up. 'Okay, we're outta here.'

Reynolds raised his hands. 'Sorry, excuse me. That was uncalled for. Please, sir have a seat.'

Shack looked at Amanda. She nodded. He sat down.

'Thank you. Okay . . . Let's get back to last night. The woman on the bridge. You got a phone call to meet her.'

Shack pointed to the folders on the table. 'Everything we have to say is already in our statements, Chief Inspector. There's nothing else we can add.'

Reynolds put his hand on the folder. 'Yes of course, but you asked if there's a connection. Well there seems to be something.'

Shack adjusted his eye-patch. 'You think we might get to it before we're much older?'

'The woman on the bridge . . . you said she called herself Anna Seranova. The same family name as your deceased friend in Devon.'

Amanda frowned. 'Where are you going with this, Chief Inspector?'

'The woman on the bridge was not who she said she was.'

'So who was she?'

'Her name is . . . was, Ludmilla Sokolova. A Ukrainian national. She'd been in the UK for almost six months. Apparently working as an interpreter at the Ukrainian Embassy. And initial background checks don't show anything other than she was here doing exactly what she was supposed to . . . Interpreting.'

Amanda shook her head slightly. 'I'm sorry I don't follow?'

'Ludmilla Sokolova was nothing more than an interpreter, Miss Lang. Not a spy. Not a terrorist. Not on any watch-list. Never been in any trouble at home. Never had any issues while here in the UK.'

'And your point, Chief Inspector?'

'My point is . . .Why would a seemingly ordinary interpreter, with no criminal history want to kill you two?'

Chapter Thirty One
'Wretched'

The interview with Reynolds, although polite, was definitely charged and the tension between Shack and the DCI tangible. Amanda could sense Shack's lingering annoyance, hence the reason she'd taken him into the first pub they came across.

'Come on, partner I'm buying you a nice lunch.'

The Hammersmith Arms was busy with the lunch-time trade. As they entered a table became free right by the door. They took their seats and looked at the menu.

'Steak pie and chips for me.'

Amanda stood up. 'You want a beer or something stronger?'

'Stella's fine thanks, luv.'

She went to the bar and ordered the food, returning with the drinks.

Shack was looking out of the window when she got back to the table.

Amanda said, 'This should put a smile on your face.'

'Great.' He picked up the pint and tapped her glass. 'Cheers, Y'Ladyship.'

She nodded towards the window. 'What's so interesting out there?'

Shack discreetly pointed to the person coming through the door. It was Detective Constable Peers.

Being seated next to the entrance, Shack and Amanda were hard to miss. As he entered Peers raised his hand and smiled. 'Hi.'

Amanda returned the smile.

Shack frowned. 'If you're surveilling us detective, you might want to work on your cover tactics.

Peers smile remained. 'No, sir. I'm just in for some lunch. Can I get you guys a drink?'

* * *

In Saint Thomas's Hospital, PC Tony Robson had been on shift since 6am. Boredom had set in hours ago and he was finding it difficult to stay awake in the warm ICU area. For the fourth time that day he got up from his chair and went to the vending machine. The coffee was disgusting, but it did give him the tiny shot of caffeine he craved. As he strolled back to his position in front of Sir Rowland Deveraux's room, the alarms began bleeping. Two nurses rushed past him almost knocking the coffee from his hand. He quickly returned to his post and through the open door could see Deveraux convulsing. A doctor appeared and dashed into the room followed by another nurse. Robson watched as the medical team tried to calm their patient and extubate the breathing tube.

As one of the nurses came out the young copper asked, 'Is he okay, nurse?'

'He'll be fine now,' she nodded and rushed off.

PC Robson put down his coffee and removed the phone from his stab-vest. He tapped the screen and waited. 'Robson, seven-five-nine-one. Yes . . . Inspector Murray, please . . . Afternoon, sir . . . Yes, Sir Rowland has just come out of the coma . . . Yes sir, of course.'

As he hung up Lady Deveraux appeared with the nurse. After days of waiting around the hospital the stress was clearly visible. She certainly looked a lot less elegant than when she had arrived.

The nurse stopped her going in. 'Please wait, Your Ladyship. We're just finishing off. You can come in shortly.'

The police constable smiled and pointed to his chair. 'Would you like a seat, Lady Deveraux?'

She raised her hand and began pacing the corridor. Robson sat down and drank his coffee. Several minutes later the medical team came out.

'How is my husband, doctor?'

'Well he's out of the coma as you can see. So that's good. We're going to do some more toxicology tests and we'll continue with the antibiotics and fluids. I'll have another look at him this evening.'

'Thank you, doctor. May I see him now?'

'Yes, of course. But just a few minutes. He's still very weak.'

She smiled. 'Still weak . . . All right . . . Thank you, doctor.'

PC Robson watched as she entered the room and slowly closed the door.

Deveraux was ashen. The bloodshot eyes had dark bags below them. A couple of days stubble showed on his chin. His hair was matted with sweat.

Lady Deveraux took his hand gently. 'Oh, my dear, you do look a sight. How are you feeling?'

The look on the man's face said it all. His voice croaked. 'I feel absolutely wretched, old girl.'

She leaned down. 'Wretched? . . . you feel wretched? . . . Oh dear.' She leaned in closer. 'Wait until I get you home, Rowland. Then you'll know what wretched really is!'

Chapter Thirty Two
'Mister Cool'

The walk from the pub took them a little over twenty minutes. They chatted most of the way but fell silent as they passed the shooting location. The police cordon was still in place on Hammersmith Bridge. A couple of inquisitive tourists intent on taking pictures were moved on by the young copper on guard. It was late afternoon by the time they entered Amanda's flat.

'You want another drink?' asked Shack.

'No thank you! . . . I need a coffee after that little session.'

He laughed. 'Lightweight . . . Okay, I'll make you a coffee.'

A few minutes later they were out on the balcony. Amanda sipped at her coffee. Shack drank from a bottle of Stella.

'You were a little tense this morning, darling.'

He turned and frowned. 'Tense?'

'In the interview. You're usually chilled, but not this morning.'

'Yeah . . . maybe. It's just that I've heard of him before.'

'Him?'

He took a mouthful of beer, then said, 'DCI Reynolds . . . When I was with the Met, he was only a Detective Sergeant, but he climbed through the ranks.'

'And that's a problem for you because?'

Shack stood up and waved the empty bottle. 'Gonna get another of these. You want anything?'

She shook her head.

A few moments later he sat down again. Amanda looked at him 'Well?'

'What?'

'Reynolds?'

Shack frowned. 'The word was, he didn't have a problem fitting-up suspects. His conviction rate was one of the best in the Met. A couple were overturned on appeal, but that still didn't affect his rise to stardom. I heard he's destined for Deputy Chief Constable.'

'Did you ever have any dealing with him?'

'Not directly, but he'll have checked us out. Especially me being ex job.'

She smiled. 'Now I understand.' She put her hand on his. 'Forget Reynolds. Can I have Mister Cool back, please?'

He laughed and raised his bottle in a mock toast. 'Yes, ma'am. Mister Cool it is.'

'Do you want anything to eat, darling?'

'No thanks, luv, I'm good.'

Amanda finished her coffee. 'Right, partner . . . our next move. Today's wasted, so we'll head north tomorrow.'

'No problem. You're the boss, Y'Ladyship.'

'And I think we should get away early . . . beat the traffic?'

He nodded. 'Okay.'

'Leave about six-thirty then?'

Shack groaned. 'Oh goody . . . I love early mornings.'

Chapter Thirty Three
'The A1 North'

Shack was already awake when his phone-alarm beeped. He could hear Amanda's shower.

'Okay, Y'Ladyship I'm up,' he said quietly.

He quickly showered and shaved, then stuffed a few things in a holdall. Amanda was in the kitchen, a slice of toast and honey in her hand when he entered.

She smiled. 'Morning, darling,' then pushed a plate with a bacon sandwich across to him.

'Mornin, luv.'

She poured his tea. 'All ready to go, partner?'

He nodded as he munched on the sandwich. 'Not sure we need to stay up there though.' He swallowed a mouthful of tea. 'But you could be right. Best to be ready.'

* * *

They headed out of the city and joined the A1 just after Edgeware. The traffic heading into London was heavy. The northbound side was busy but moved swiftly and they made good time. Amanda drove fast. Shack liked that about her. He trusted her behind the wheel, something he'd never been able to do with anyone since the crash that killed his family.

He put the seat back and relaxed as the Evoque ate up the miles. He took out his phone and swiped the screen. Two days ago they'd copied the diary and journal transcripts to the *Cloud* and were now able to access them on their smartphones. The actual diary and journal, along with the transcripts, had been secured in a locked document case and couriered over to Lambert & Arnold, along with a letter to Carlton Lambert. In the event they did not collect the case in seven days he was to give it to Detective Chief Inspector Reynolds at Hammersmith Station.

Shack swiped through the transcript. 'I gotta hand it to you, Y'Ladyship.' He held up the phone. 'Working this out was very cool.'

She glanced sideways and smiled. 'I was always good at cryptic crosswords. And there's this thing called Google, darling. '

He pointed to the screen. 'Right . . . But this isn't a crossword, luv.' He sat up and began reading . . . *Two hellish creatures mayhem make, within the house of God. An angel comes, their mischief ends, beneath his golden rod. While one escapes the other stays to wear a stonelike frown. From column top, with impish grin, forever will look down. And look upon the angel's choir, beneath the seat a heart of fire.'*

He switched off the phone, straightened the eye-patch and eased back in his seat.

Amanda glanced across. 'Why the smile?'

'Just thinking, luv. You have to hand it to that Captain Volodin. He was one smart Russian.'

She also smiled. 'And not a bad poet.'

A few miles north of Newark they turned off the A1 and onto the A46.

Amanda pointed to the SATNAV. 'Not long now.'

* * *

On the top deck Konstantine Mirov and Ivan Permyak enjoyed the sea breeze as the *Angelina* ploughed through the calm sea. Konni stood at the rail intent on the distant coastline as it slipped past. Ivan though, was focussed on his iPad.

Konni went into the bridge and nodded to the helmsman, then turned to the captain. 'Morning, Rustam. How are we doing?'

'Morning, boss. Making good time.' He went over to the digital displays and pointed to one of the larger screens. 'Currently making thirty-five knots.'

The boss nodded. 'Good. And ETA?'

The captain looked at the screen again. 'On location approximately sixteen-hundred hours.'

Konni smiled. 'Excellent, thank you captain.' As he turned to leave the bridge he patted the helmsman on the back.

On deck, Ivan was still fully focussed on the iPad screen.

'So, where are they, brother?'

Ivan looked up, smiled, and held up the tablet. Like a lecturer in front of his class he pointed to the screen. 'They have now just turned from A1, brother.'

Chapter Thirty Four
'Three Danish'

Fifteen minutes after joining the A46 they turned right onto the Saxilby Road. A couple of miles further on they looked at each other and smiled. The imposing twin towers of Lincoln Cathedral could be seen in the distance.

As they passed the ornate WELCOME TO LINCOLN sign Shack looked at his watch. 'Just over three and a half hours. Not bad going, Y'Ladyship.'

The closer they got to the city centre the heavier the traffic became. The streets looked to be filled with locals and tourists. 'Ever been here before?' said Amanda

He shook his head 'No. But it looks an interesting place. Lot of great old buildings.'

'Two thousand years ago it was a Roman stronghold. Later, when the Normans arrived they developed it into a major mediaeval city. It has a lot of history.'

Shack grinned. 'As long as it's got what we're looking for, luv.'

She shook her head, then turned off into the main carpark.

As they walked out on to the busy street, Amanda said, 'I really need a coffee.'

'Okay. Let's see if we can get somewhere a bit closer.'

They walked uphill towards the cathedral and found a nice tea-room directly opposite the *Visitors Centre*. There were a couple of free tables outside.

Shack pulled out a chair for Amanda. 'This okay?'

'Yes fine. Order me a coffee and a Danish or something . . . I'll be right back.'

He stood for a second and watched as she went over to the *Visitors Centre*.

A waitress arrived. 'Good morning, sir.'

He smiled. 'Mornin. Just a sec let me look at the menu.'

The girl waited.

'Okay . . . a pot of tea, a large coffee and two Danish pastries, please.'

'Thank you, sir.'

As she turned to go, he said, 'Better make that three Danish, luv.'

A couple of minutes later the waitress returned with a large tray. As she unloaded their order Amanda arrived. She stood back until the girl had finished, then took her seat.

'I'm ready for this . . . And you got me two Danish . . . yummy.'

'Oh . . . right, yeah.'

The disappointed look on his face made her laugh. 'I'm joking.'

He poured the tea and nodded to the brochures. 'Visitors guides. Good idea.'

On the west side of the square two men stood in front of a gift shop. One never took his eyes off Shack and Amanda. The other tapped out a WhatsApp message . . . *They have stopped in café near church.*

Chapter Thirty Five
'The Imp'

Since its construction almost a thousand years ago, it has borne many names. But today it is widely accepted that the magnificent structure in the centre of the city, is known only as *Lincoln Cathedral*. With over five-thousand square metres of floor space it is the fourth largest cathedral in the United Kingdom and puritans of gothic architecture regard it as the best example.

Amanda and Shack joined the queue at the main door. A large party of young school children jostled each other in their excitement to enter. The kids' progress however was slowed by a bunch of camera-mad Japanese snapping away at the wonderful arched entrance.

A mildly authoritative, 'Move forward, please,' from the burly warden, cleared the Japanese log-jam and the small crowd moved into the foyer area.

A few steps forward they entered the magnificent vaulted nave. Shack stood with his mouth open as he looked up to the roof. 'Oh, my God! . . . This is . . . awesome.'

Amanda stood silent at his side, overwhelmed by the beauty of the amazing building.

Other visitors walked around them as they slowly made their way into the centre of the enormous cathedral. They were twenty yards in before they looked at the Visitors Guide. Shack took her arm and moved away from the main body of the nave. They found a quiet place next to one of the huge supporting columns and opened the brochure. Amanda took out her phone and swiped the screen. The transcript from Captain Volodin's journal came up. She scrolled through and found the passage she was looking for. She looked around for a second or two, then at Shack.

'*Two creatures come to the cathedral.* That could mean animals, demons or ghosts *and cause mayhem . . .* Anything in the guide like that?'

Shack rubbed his eye, then flicked through the pages. 'How about this? *The Legend of the Lincoln Imp.* Two imps . . . whatever they are, come to the cathedral to cause mischief. But an angel comes to chase them out. One escapes and the other is turned to stone.'

Amanda moved closer, her voice almost a whisper. 'That's it, partner.'

He grinned and pointed to her phone. 'What else?'

Amanda quietly read the rest of the cryptic poem . . . '*From column top, with impish grin, forever will look down. And look upon the angel's choir, beneath the seat a heart of fire.*'

Shack flipped over more pages. 'Here you go . . *The Angels Choir.*'

She looked at the photographs. 'Right . . . says it's the upper part of the *East Transept.*' She looked up and nodded to the far end of the building. 'Down there.'

He slipped his arm through hers. 'Let's go, Y'Ladyship.'

They made their way down to the intersection where the East-West transept crossed the North-South. The morning sun beamed in through the fabulous *Rose Window,* sending a kaleidoscope of colour onto the astonished visitors below.

As they moved towards the *East Transept* Amanda pointed up to the magnificent carved angels looking down from each sides of the structure. '*The Angels Choir.*'

Shack smiled and pointed to the top of one of the magnificent columns. 'And I guess that ugly little bugger is the Imp?'

Amanda nodded and stared at the tiny gargoyle. The creature, legs crossed in defiance, mouth open in a toothless-grin, forever looked down on the people below.

Shack turned around. 'So where is he looking?'

Amanda swiped the phone's screen and read quietly . . . '*And look upon the angels choir, beneath the seat a heart of fire.*'

'A seat like a heart? Or a fire? What?'

She pointed to the rows of ornately carved choir stalls. 'Seats.'

'It's roped off up there.'

She winked. 'We'll have to be quick then.'

They looked around for stewards or clergy. None. Only the dozens of captivated visitors wandered admiringly around. No one paid them any attention as the good-looking woman and the one eyed man unclipped the thick blue rope and stepped up onto the choristers' area.

Shack moved to go to the right, but Amanda said quietly. 'This side. This is where the Imp is looking.'

There were three tiers of beautifully carved choir stalls each side of the central aisle. Shack took the back tier, Amanda the front. They moved slowly along the rows checking each seat.

136

A couple of minutes later they arrived at the end nearest the alter. 'Anything?' said Amanda.

He shook his head. 'Middle tier then.'

Together they moved down the centre row, each seat checked twice. Again, a minute or two later, they arrived back at their starting point. They looked at each other and smiled. Carved into the ancient oak of the first seat was a small ornate heart surrounded by flames.

'*A heart of fire*,' said Shack.

Amanda looked towards the nave and saw a young clergyman approaching. He was making his way through the crowded area towards them. 'Be quick, I'll stall him.'

Shack knelt down and searched below the seat. Nothing. He felt around the polished wooden floorboards for anything loose. Nothing.

Amanda was back on the other side of the blue rope as the curate arrived. He smiled. 'I'm sorry, miss, but the high altar and choristery are out of bounds.'

She returned the smile. 'Yes, I'm sorry Father. We're very naughty. But many years ago my friend used to sing in the King's Choir here,' her smile broadened. 'Apparently that was his old seat. He just wanted to see it again.'

The curate was about to speak when Shack unclipped the rope. 'Sorry, padre, I . . .'

Amanda touched his arm. 'I was just saying how you used to sing here, Tom. And how much you wanted to see your old seat again.'

Shack grinned. 'Yes . . that's right. Me a choirboy . . . who'd have thought it?'

The young curate looked at them both, focusing for a second on Shack's eye-patch. 'Well I suppose there's no harm done.'

'And I'll make sure he leaves a generous donation when we leave, Father.'

'That's very kind. Bless you.'

As the young man walked away Amanda turned to Shack. 'Well?'

He linked his arm through hers. 'Yes . . . Now let's get outta here.'

Chapter Thirty Six
'Demeter'

Their excitement was tangible as they quickly wove in and out along the crowded pavement, Amanda's curiosity growing with every step.

'Where was it? Whatever it is?'

'Let's get back to the car.'

It took a little less than ten minutes to get to the car park. The lights flashed as Amanda flipped the locks. The morning sun had made the interior uncomfortably warm, so she started the engine and switched on the air-conditioning.

'So what have we got?'

Shack reached under his jacket and took out a small nondescript leather folder, about the size of an ordinary envelope. The once soft brown material had dried and cracked but the flap, secured with a thin leather thong, was still intact.

For several seconds they looked at the object. Reverently Shack turned it around in his hands, examining the small innocuous item. He took a tissue from the glove box and gently cleaned off a hundred years of dust.

'Where was it?'

'Underneath at the back. Where the floor rises to the rear tier. Pushed into an old ventilation slot.'

Carefully he undid the fastening and eased open the flap. He looked at Amanda, then even more carefully removed the contents. The paper was of the finest quality. Shack unfolded the document and frowned. 'Russian!'

Amanda put on her glasses and took the letter from him. 'Let's see what we have?'

For several minutes she studied the fine handwritten Cyrillic. She picked up her handbag and took out a small notebook and pen. 'Right, let's see if I can make this out?'

Shack watched in silent admiration as she worked on the translation.

At last she looked up and smiled. 'I think this is right, but I may need to check a couple of phrases later.'

'Come on then, Y'Ladyship. Let's hear it.'

'Okay, but bear with me . . . *We journeyed as Demeter did till claw-like rocks she found.*
In darkest night from sea-soaked decks did leap the devil's hound. Where growled the beast in hallowed halls above the silver bays. Between night's arms, as daylight dawns, the noble lady lays.'

Shack's excitement waned. 'And that means what?'

She shook her head slightly. 'Not sure yet.'

'So what d'you think? Back to London?'

Again she shook her head. She continued to look at the translation. 'No . . . Let's find somewhere a bit more comfortable and have a think.'

'The hotel we passed on our way in?'

Amanda handed him the notebook then fastened her seatbelt. 'Sounds good.'

They left the carpark and took the Saxilby Road back to the A46. A few miles further on they pulled into the carpark of *Damon's Hotel.*

The hotel looked to be busy with some sort of conference. Lots of men and women in business suits wandered in and out of the Reception area. The lounge was very busy but the bar reasonably quiet.

Shack grinned and nodded to the bar. 'Now how convenient is that?'

Amanda frowned disapprovingly. 'Maybe we should leave the celebrating until we know what we have here, darling?' She patted her handbag.

'Spoilsport.'

They took a table in the corner overlooking the rear gardens.

The barman came from behind his counter. 'Good morning, guys.'

Shack looked up. 'Pot of tea and a coffee, please.'

'Anything to eat?'

'Not just yet, thanks.'

Amanda already had her glasses on and was studying the translation. Shack looked around the room. A young man and woman sat in the other corner. Two businessmen were having a sneaky one at the bar. One old chap a couple of tables away was reading his paper.

He leaned closer to her. 'Anything I can do to help?'

She moved her chair nearer to him and quietly read through the translation, line by line.

He adjusted his eye-patch then stretched his arms above his head. 'I need the loo.' As he stood up he said, 'That name. *Demeter* . . . don't know who that is, but it rings a bell.'

As Shack passed the old guy's table the man looked over his paper. 'Dracula!'

Shack turned. 'Sorry?'

The man lowered the paper. 'You said *Demeter.*'

Shack nodded. 'Yeah?'

'*Demeter* is not a who, it's a what.'

Shack began to smile. 'Go on.'

'*The Demeter* was the ship that brought Dracula to England, in Bram Stoker's novel.'

Shack's smile turned into a large grin. 'Thank you, sir.'

The man nodded and continued reading his paper.

Shack went back to their table. 'Did you hear that?'

Amanda nodded and took out her iPad.

'I'll be right back.'

As he walked away, she tapped the name *Dracula,* into the search bar.

A few minutes later Shack returned. Amanda had poured his tea and was drinking her coffee.

'So?' he said.

She drank a little more coffee then picked up her glasses. She held up the tablet . . . 'This is an extract from Bram Stoker's novel.' She began reading . . . '*In 1885 the Russian Schooner The Demeter was hit by a wild storm and ran aground in Whitby harbour. Mysteriously all the crew were dead including the captain who was lashed to the helm. The instant The Demeter ran aground a huge black dog was seen to leap ashore and run up the hill towards Whitby Abbey. Dracula had arrived in England!*'

Shack frowned. 'So the message is about bloody Dracula? . . . Pardon the pun.'

She shook her head. 'No. It's about the location.'

'Location?'

'Finish your tea . . . We're going to Whitby.'

Chapter Thirty Seven
'Spooky Voice'

The distance on the SATNAV read 105 miles. The route took them onto the A15 directly north to the Humber Bridge then into the North Yorkshire Moors. Arrival in Whitby was 14:38.

'You sure you don't want me to drive, luv?'

'No I'm fine, darling.'

Shack eased back in his seat. 'Okay . . . So we get there and what?'

'Can you bring up Captain Volodin's journal transcript?'

Shack took out his phone and swiped the screen. 'Right, what am I looking for?'

'Scroll to the part where he leaves Russia.'

'Hold on . . . Right, got it . . . He leaves Moscow in an old cart with the five children, the five trunks. The Tsar's treasure. Once out of the city he gets hold of a truck and heads north to Saint Petersburg. From there he takes ship across the Baltic, around Denmark and across the North Sea.'

'Right. But it doesn't tell us where the ship lands in England.'

Shack picked up her notebook. 'And that's where the cryptic message in the Cathedral comes in.'

'Yes. Look at the translation I did earlier.'

Shack opened the book and read out loud . . . *'We journeyed as Demeter did till claw-like rocks she found. In darkest . . . '*

'Just a second. There it is . . . His journey was the same as *The Demeter*. And we know from Stoker's novel that *The Demeter* foundered in Whitby Bay. Which means Volodin landed at Whitby.'

Shack looked at her and grinned. 'You're sure this is kosher? Dracula? Whitby? And a plan based on a fictitious book?'

'Yes . . . The message you found today was thanks to Volodin's cryptic poem in his journal.' She tapped her notebook. 'Why should this one be any less viable?'

'Okay, I'll buy it. But what're we looking for when we get there?'

'Read the rest of the message.'

In a spooky voice, Shack read aloud . . . *'In darkest night from sea-soaked decks did leap the devil's hound. Where growled the beast in hallowed halls above the silver bays.'*

'Stop there a second. Let me think . . . Hallowed halls . . . Hallowed halls . . . Another cathedral or church?'

Shack looked out of the window and watched the fields fly past. 'I doubt there's a cathedral in Whitby, luv. But there must be a few churches . . . And there's the old Abbey on the hilltop.'

She turned for a second and smiled. 'That's it . . . *Hallowed halls above the silver bays. Above the bays* must be the hilltop. The Abbey on the hilltop.'

He turned in his seat to face her. 'Okay, okay, I'm still buying this. So we get to the Abbey and then?'

'Read the next line.'

The spooky voice returned. *'Between night's arms, as daylight dawns, the noble lady lays.'*

She turned for a second and frowned. 'Think I'll have to get back to you on that.'

* * *

Shack was driving now. The sun was warm and the road quiet. Radio 2 churned out an old Soul classic that made him smile. He turned to look at her for a second . . . she was sleeping. As his eyes turned back to the road the truck ploughed into them . . . The horrendous sound of metal on metal as the heavy vehicle destroyed the front of their car. . . The flames grew quickly engulfing the interior. She was unconscious . . . he screamed as he tried to free her from the inferno. Then pain in his arm . . .

'Shack, Shack,' shouted Amanda.

'Oh, Jesus!'

'Are you okay, darling? You were dreaming . . . screaming.'

'Sorry, luv.' He sat up and wiped the sweat from his face, lowered the window and sucked in a lung full of fresh air . . . 'I'm okay now. Sorry.'

'You still have the crash nightmare?'

He nodded and closed the window. 'Not as often, but it's still there.'

'Do you want to stop for a while? Get a drink?'

He shook his head. 'No, it's okay.'

'Are you sure?'

He sighed and nodded. 'Yeah, fine, luv. How much further?'

'We crossed the Humber Bridge thirty minutes ago. Little bit less than an hour now.'

He rubbed his arm. 'Bloody hell that's sore.'

'Oh, yes, sorry about that. I couldn't wake you.'

'So you thumped me?'

She turned to him for a second. 'Well, yes. Sorry, darling.'

Chapter Thirty Eight
'Whitby'

Situated at the mouth of the River Esk, Whitby is a town and port on England's East coast. From the middle ages the main industry had been fishing and whaling. But in the 1800's and with the development of the railways, tourism became the main source of income for the quaint Yorkshire location. The town's most famous feature, located high above the town on *East Cliff,* is the imposing Gothic ruin of *Whitby Abbey*.

The main road into town was busy. The summer always brought the tourist trade and the lovely harbour and old ruin were two of the main attractions. Shack and Amanda drove down into the centre, across the *Swing Bridge*, then up the hill towards the Abbey. At the top the main road continued south. A T-junction led to a smaller road on the left. The old sign said *Church Lane.* Another more contemporary notice pointed, unnecessarily, to the Abbey. The magnificent old ruin was now in full view. Imposing, beautiful and sinister and with its prominent hilltop position it was clear to see why it attracted so much interest and attention, the Dracula legend notwithstanding.

There was, and rightly so, no carpark in the vicinity of the Abbey. The nearest was signposted as a mile away to the south. Several owners had foolishly taken the liberty of parking along *Church Lane*, an action they would soon regret as a rather rotund female traffic warden was happily doling out tickets to the offending vehicles.

A small tearoom and gift shop provided a few parking spaces at the side. Shack pointed to a Mini backing out. 'Lucky white heather.'

Amanda pulled up, then quickly reversed into the vacant spot. She switched off the engine and sighed. 'I am really in need of a tall glass of wine, mister.'

As they stepped out Shack nodded to the tearoom. 'You might just have to settle for a coffee, luv.'

The place was busy but there were a couple of tables free. They took a tiny two seater next to the window. 'Coffee?' said Shack.

He went to the counter and saw the small bottles of wine in the chiller. 'A bottle of that Pino please and two bottles of the red.'

Back at the table he poured the wine into her glass. She smiled. 'Oh, how good does that look?'

They chinked glasses. 'Cheers. You did a great job driving today, Y'Ladyship.'

She took a mouthful of Pino. 'Mmmm.'

He smiled at her enjoyment of the cheap wine. 'So . . . We're here. Any thoughts on what's next?'

She leaned across the little table. 'I have. But we're not going to be able to do much today.'

'No?'

She gestured to the dozens of tourists wandering up and down to the Abbey. 'Too many people about, darling.' She took another drink. 'And I think we need to be here in the morning.'

He frowned. 'The morning?'

She picked up her handbag and took out the notebook. No-one, other than a little girl fascinated by Shack's eye-patch, was paying them any attention. She opened the book 'We were stuck on the last line.'

Shack nodded. 'Yeah.'

She quietly read through her translation of the Cathedral message. *'Between night's arms, as daylight dawns, the noble lady lays.'*

Again he nodded. 'Okay?'

'As daylight dawns.' She smiled. 'We need to be here when the sun comes up.'

'Right, I'm buying it again . . . And?'

She pointed to the words in the book. 'And what if *nights arms* is nothing to do with nighttime?'

Shack poured his second bottle of red and shrugged. 'How d'you mean?'

'What if *night,* is actually *knight* as in mediaeval knights of old?'

For several seconds he said nothing . . . then leaned forward, took hold of her hand and kissed it. 'Genius!'

Chapter Thirty Nine
'An Exciting Town'

The Dolphin Hotel was situated on the east side of the Esk, a little way along the promenade from the *Swing Bridge*. Amanda pulled into the rear carpark. 'This looks really nice.'

Shack took their overnight bags from the back of the Evoque. 'Good call, Y'Ladyship.'

The lights flashed as she locked the car. She linked her arm through his and they headed round to the front of the hotel.

At reception a very pleasant older lady greeted them. 'Good afternoon.'

Shack dropped the bags. 'Hi. We don't have a reservation, but we do need a room, please.'

The lady smiled and looked at her computer screen. 'We have a double on the top floor.'

'Have you a twin?'

She looked again. 'There's a family room on the front overlooking the river.'

'Sounds perfect. Thank you.'

Shack dropped her bag on the bed. 'You have the double, luv. You've earned it today.'

She went to the window and looked out over the busy promenade. Both sides of the river had tourists and locals going about their business and enjoying the early summer weather. 'Oh, look. The bridge is opening.'

Shack joined her. Together they watched as the *Swing Bridge did exactly what it said on the tin.* Swing open. They watched as a sleek motor launch sailed past and out to the sea.

'That's probably as exciting as it's going to get here, Y'Ladyship.'

She frowned and shook her head. 'Now don't be unkind. I'm sure it's a very exciting little town.'

'Er, okay. I believe you. So what's the plan, luv? Shower and a walk round the town. Find somewhere nice to eat?'

She kissed his cheek. 'Sounds perfect, darling.' Then she picked up her bag and went into the bathroom.

He turned back to the window and grinned. 'Don't know how I'm going to contain myself.'

They left the hotel a little after five o'clock. The promenades on both sides of the Esk were still busy and the cafes and bars along the river-walk were bustling.

'So, Y'Ladyship, what's it to be?'

She linked her arm through his and headed towards the *Swing Bridge.* 'How about a little walk to stretch our legs, then a drink and some food down at the harbour?'

'Sounds like a plan, luv.'

After crossing to the west side of the river they sauntered along the promenade and down towards the old port. The distance from the hotel to the harbour wasn't far, but they took their time and enjoyed the cool evening breeze coming in off the sea.

As they turned the corner Amanda suddenly stopped and pointed to a hanging pub-sign. 'Now this is the place for us, darling.'

Shack looked up and grinned. 'Ain't that the truth.'

The colourful sign depicted a bearded man wearing a large floppy hat. One eye was covered with a black patch and below, in olde-worlde script announced, *The Pirate*.

'Looks like the right place for a good drink with my fellow buccaneers, Y'Ladyship.'

'I'm afraid we won't be doing too much buccaneering, darling. We have another early start in the morning.'

Shack held open the door for her . . . and groaned.

Chapter Forty
'The Graveyard'

The Abbey's medieval graveyard was located a hundred yards inland from the west transept and shielded from the road by a small wooded area. It was almost 4am when Amanda pulled the Evoque off *Church Lane* and into the shadow of the trees.

Shack looked at his watch. 'Maybe half an hour. How're you feeling, Y'Ladyship?'

She looked through the trees, up to the ghostly ruin. 'Nervous. Excited. Concerned.'

'Why concerned, luv?'

'If we're right about what we think is here, we could end up being tomb raiders or grave robbers.'

'That's a bit harsh, Y'Ladyship.'

She looked back to the ruin. 'Either way it's got to be a little sacrilegious.'

Inland to the west, the sky was still as black as pitch, but out across the North Sea the horizon was already visible as the sun's rays lightened the day.

Shack took a bottle of Coke from the glovebox and offered it to Amanda.

Her eyes were still fixed on the mysterious abbey. 'No thank you.'

He cracked the cap and swallowed half the contents. 'I could do with a beer.'

She turned to him and shook her head slightly. 'Seriously?'

He grinned. 'Okay, a cuppa tea then.'

He finished the Coke and dropped the empty over the back of his seat. The sun breached the horizon and the sky was filled with golden rays. The graveyard was still in shadow, the old stone markers ghoul-like in the fading darkness

Shack took the flashlight from the door-well. 'Right, partner. Shall we?'

They left the wooded area and entered the cemetery, their intrusion an invitation for the blackbirds to begin their morning overture. It was still cool, but the fast-rising sun warmed the air. With the aid of the torch they made their way between the gravestones, the sun getting higher every minute. A few moments later they reached the far wall. The skeleton of the abbey's west transept cast long ghostly shadows over the uneven rows of grave markers.

They leaned against the wall and Shack switched off the torch. Amanda linked her arm through his. They stood in silence and waited. She looked over her shoulder and watched as the sun rose higher, its rays chasing the darkness from the cemetery. It was almost four-thirty when the first beams shot through the imposing structure.

Shack pointed to the top of the ruin, to where the rose-window used to be. 'Look!'

The sun climbed higher and then, like some movie special effect, a golden shaft beamed through the opening and fell on the centre of the graveyard.

Amanda turned and smiled. 'Come on!'

They quickly made their way in and out of the markers, the warm sun at their backs. Almost at the centre of the cemetery the shaft of light had illuminated three ancient stone slabs.

Amanda put her hand to her mouth. 'Oh, my God.'

Shack knelt at the left grave and cleared away the covering of moss. 'Sir Egbert Waldren.'

Amanda worked on the right hand slab. 'And here we have, Sir Godwin De Plessey.'

They looked at each other and laughed. The grass, damp with morning dew, made their knees wet. Their hands were filthy with the business of clearing the moss, yet they still laughed.

'Between knight's arms,' said Amanda, 'as daylight dawns . . .'

'The noble lady lays,' said Shack.

They moved to the centre stone and together began clearing the weeds and moss. The carved inscription was illegible, worn away with centuries of northern weather.

'I can't make anything out,' she said.

He nodded. 'No problem . . . Let's see if we can get this off.'

Together they pushed at the corner of the granite slab.

Shack groaned. 'It's not moving.' He changed position and sat on the grass, his back pressed hard against Sir Egbert's grave. Using his legs to gain purchase, he strained at the huge chunk of rock.

Amanda joined him and together they pushed at the ancient covering. A few moments later the grating noise of stone on stone shattered the morning's silence.

'That's it . . . That's it . . . It's going!'

As the heavy slab slipped from position the sound of someone clapping startled them. They quickly got to their feet and turned to see Count Oleg Stranski. Two younger men stood close behind. The Count stopped applauding and smiled.

'Well done both of you. I knew all along you would find it.'

Shack frowned. 'Count Stranski . . . Oleg . . .What're you doing here?'

Still smiling, the old man moved forward a little. 'We are here to help you, my boy.'

Amanda raised her hand to shield her eyes from the sun. 'Help us? How on earth did you know we were here?'

'Don't worry, my dear . . .We'll get to that. So, shall we get it out?' He made a slight hand gesture and said something in Russian. The two men moved to the open grave. His smile returned as he came closer. 'Stand back, my dears. These chaps will have it out in no time.'

Shack looked at Amanda then watched as the two men struggled to pull the heavy steamer trunk from the dark hole. Stranski snapped something in Russian and one of the men jumped down into the opening. Between them they managed to pull the dust-covered chest from its resting place, up over the edge, and onto the grass. Both were breathing heavily as they stood up and stepped back. The Count, wide-eyed, stared at the leather-bound coffer. He moved to the edge of the open grave.

The crack of a single gunshot echoed across the hilltop. Startled, Amanda and Shack spun round to see Ivan Permyak and four armed men walk out of the small wood. One of the men carried a rifle. A wisp of blue smoke drifted from the muzzle into the still morning air. A stern-faced Permyak pointed to the Count's men. Two of his minders rushed forward. Stranski's men were swiftly searched, their weapons confiscated.

Shack took Amanda's hand. She held on tight as the Russian approached. Permyak moved to the open grave, then grinned as he looked down on the body of Count Oleg Stranski.

He turned to them and smiled. 'This is very helpful of him to fall into hole . . . yes?'

They said nothing.

Ivan took a flash-drive from his pocket, held it up for Shack and Amanda to see, then dropped it carefully onto the dead Count's chest. He turned and smiled. 'Just because he is dead does not mean he cannot be useful . . . yes?'

More orders in Russian and the heavy slab was manoeuvred back into place, covering the old man.

Ivan looked at Amanda and Shack again. 'Yes . . . I think he is very helpful.' He turned to Stranski's men. 'And what shall we do with you guys. I don't see any more holes?'

The men began pleading for their lives. Permyak raised his hand and walked over to them. He was right in front of their faces. He spoke quietly. Amanda saw their expressions change from abject fear to blessed relief.

With a wave of his hand he said, 'Go.' As they slowly moved away, he said, 'Oh, wait.'

The men turned around. Fear back on their faces.

Ivan held out his hand. Smiling, he said, 'He won't need Bentley anymore. So I take keys.'

Chapter Forty One
'Tough Guy'

Amanda and Shack were escorted out of the graveyard and through the trees. Stranski's car was parked next to hers. A short distance away a beat up old van already had its engine running. Permyak handed the Count's keys to one of his men and exchanged a few quiet words. A minute or two later he watched as the beautiful old Bentley drove off to the south.

He turned to Amanda and held out his hand. 'And your keys please, Miss Lang.'

She purposefully tossed the fob short. The Russian frowned, then bent down and picked it up. The lights flashed as he flipped the locks.

'In the back, Miss Lang.'

She moved away. 'I'm not getting in there.'

Ivan looked puzzled. 'Is your car. Why you don't get in?'

Shack stepped in front of her and raised his hands. 'Just go . . . leave us here.'

The Russian looked at Shack's burn scars. 'You are pretty tough guy I think, Mister Shack.'

He shook his head. 'No, not me . . . but you're not taking her.'

Ivan grinned. 'You think a one-eyed man can stop us?'

'Listen, we're no threat to you. Just go. Leave us. We don't care what happened here.'

Permyak turned to his minder and said something in Russian. They both laughed.

'Mister Shack . . . If we wanted to kill you, you would already be in the hole with Stranski. Now please, Miss Lang . . . Get in.'

She climbed in the back, quickly followed by the armed minder.

Ivan nodded to Shack. 'You drive . . . tough guy.'

He got behind the wheel as Ivan went round to the passenger side, He took out a small automatic. 'Just take it easy, yes?'

They waited and watched as the heavy trunk was loaded into the rear of the old van.

As it moved away Ivan waved the automatic. 'Just follow.'

Shack looked at Amanda in the rear-view mirror, he caught her eye . . . then winked.

They continued along the lane for about two hundred yards then at the junction took the main road down into Whitby. Shack looked at his watch; ten past five. At that time of the morning there were still very few people about. A baker's van passed them as they went round the town square. As they turned towards the harbour a young female jogger, a labrador at her side, ran across the road in front of them.

A minute or two later they drove onto the quayside. Shack could see a smart motor launch moored at the end of the breakwater. Two men sat smoking on a nearby bench. As the vehicles approached the men quickly stood up. One of them jumped down into the boat, the other smiled and raised his hand to welcome the return of his comrades.

The van pulled up adjacent to the launch. Shack was told to stop a few yards behind. The man on the quayside joined the two in the van. The heavy trunk was taken out and placed at the edge of the dock above the boat. Ivan and his minder with Amanda and Shack joined the group next to the chest. The difficulty in getting the hefty coffer down into the launch became evident.

Ivan barked some instructions and two of the three jumped down onto the gently swaying deck. The other man eased the chest to the edge and slowly pushed it over. The three below took a hold. Each groaned and strained at the cumbersome deadweight.

Amanda recognised Ivan's profanities as the Russian cursed and waved his hands at the struggling men. With more curses and grunts the trunk was safely lowered to the deck of the elegant launch.

Ivan nodded towards the old metal ladder fixed to the seawall. 'Miss Lang, if you please.'

Shack stepped forward. 'I'll go first.' He climbed down, then held up a hand. 'Okay, luv. Come on.'

The sight of her backside, as she negotiated the rusty steps, was probably the best part of the three Russians' morning.

Shack watched as Ivan and the minder went back to Amanda's car. Ivan put a hand on the young guy's shoulder. It was clear he was being given instructions. The man nodded several times, then smiled. Fist-bumps were exchanged. Ivan stood and watched as the minder did a three point turn, then drove off in the Evoque. More instructions were given to the last man on the quayside, then he drove off in the old van.

Finally the Russian climbed down. He turned to Amanda and winked. 'Okay . . . we go.'

Chapter Forty Two
'Welcome Aboard'

The launch cleared the breakwater and headed out into open sea. Half a mile or so from the harbour they changed course and turned south towards the headland. Shack looked up at the Abbey ruin. From the sea it looked even more imposing as it dominated the clifftop. As the launch rounded the headland the breeze strengthened and a fine salty spray covered the occupants. Amanda took hold of Shack's arm and nodded forward. A hundred yards from the shoreline, in the lee of the cliff, the *Angelina* lay at anchor.

It only took a few minutes of bouncing across the waves to reach *Angelina's* position. The launch slowed as it approached the stern, then slowly manoeuvred alongside the rear landing-deck. Looking down from the stern-rail was Konstantin Valery Mirov.

Two deck hands held the launch securely as Amanda and Shack were helped aboard. Ivan Permyak stepped across unaided and pointed to the steps to the upper deck. 'After you.'

At the top of the companionway they were greeted by a smiling Konstantin. 'Welcome aboard *Angelina*,' and with a gracious sweep of his hand he continued, 'Please, this way.'

The queasiness Shack had felt as the fast launch bounced across the waves was now easing as there was hardly any motion at all aboard the huge super-yacht. As they entered the impressive lower saloon he said, 'So what's going on? Why are we here, Mister Mirov?'

The Russian turned. 'Konni. Please . . . call me Konni. And I shall call you, Shack. We are now friends after all.'

Amanda frowned. 'Friends?'

'Of course, Miss Amanda.'

She looked him in the eyes. 'We have been abducted, Mister Mirov.'

He shook his head and waved a finger. 'Oh no, Miss Amanda. You are our guests. And please, not Mister Mirov. Konni. Please . . . Konni. Now would you like some breakfast?'

Shack laughed. 'Breakfast! What the hell's going on here?'

Mirov raised a hand. 'Okay, breakfast later. But a drink now I think? Tea? Coffee? Vodka? No . . . Champagne I think is called for.'

'It's not even six o'clock in the morning,' said Amanda.

Konni bowed his head apologetically. 'Of course, Miss Amanda. Tea and coffee then.' He nodded to one of the flunkies who disappeared forward.

Two more men arrived with a large tarpaulin and began spreading it out over the beautiful Kashmiri carpet. Shack and Amanda moved further into the saloon as Mirov directed the spreading of the protective covering. A moment or two later Ivan Permyak arrived with his men from the launch. Two of the burlier ones struggled to manhandle the heavy trunk into the saloon. The relief on their faces was evident as they placed the dirty old chest in the centre of the tarpaulin. A third stepped forward with a set of bolt cutters. Konni snapped an instruction in

163

Russian. The man lowered the tool and stepped outside. Shack looked at Amanda. She moved closer and touched his hand. He held onto hers.

Konstantin turned and smiled. 'We are not yet ready to open your discovery my friends.'

Chapter Forty Three
'Covert Business'

'Excuse me, sir.' The man speaking wore an immaculate white shirt; the epaulettes on his shoulders bore four gold stripes.

'Yes, Captain?'

'The motor launch has been stowed and we're ready to get underway.'

Konni nodded. 'Thank you, Rustam. Let's go.'

'Yes, sir.'

'What's our ETA?'

'Nineteen-hundred hours.'

'Perfect . . . And please arrange the transfer.'

'Of course, sir.'

As the Captain left, the steward arrived with a large tray. He placed it on the table, then arranged glasses, cups, saucers, pots of tea and coffee.

Konni touched him on the shoulder. 'That's fine, thank you. We'll manage.'

Ivan pointed to the couch. 'Mister Shack, Miss Amanda . . . Please have a seat. What would you like? Tea or coffee?'

Neither spoke. Ivan smiled. 'You really don't want anything?'

Shack leaned forward. 'Actually I could murder some tea.'

Ivan grinned. 'There will be no murders here today. For you, Miss Amanda?'

'Coffee . . . please.'

The two Russians helped themselves to drinks, then sat opposite their guests.

'Now,' said Konni, 'where to begin?'

Amanda took a drink of the excellent coffee, then looked at Ivan. 'Perhaps why you killed Count Oleg this morning?'

'Ah yes, your friend Count Oleg,' said Ivan.

Konni topped-up his tea then offered more to Shack.

'No thanks.'

'More coffee, Miss Amanda?'

She shook her head.

They heard the faint sound of the ships engines starting up. This was followed a few seconds later by the sound of the anchors being drawn.

Konni looked out of the large picture window and said to no one in particular, 'Away at last.'

He turned and remained standing. Then, as if about to present a lecture to a class, began. 'Your friend Count Stranski I'm afraid, is not one of the Russian aristocracy, Miss Amanda. He came to England in the early nineties, soon after the collapse of the Soviet Union and arrived in London as the old regime was breaking up . . . But you must of course remember, the old regime was the foundation for the new regime.' He looked at Ivan and smiled, Ivan nodded at the observation.

'Rebranding at its finest,' said Amanda.

Konni looked at her. 'Indeed . . . You see the lovely old gentleman you know as Count Oleg has, for the last thirty years, been conducting all kinds of covert business in your country.'

'Covert business?' said Shack.

The Russian nodded. 'Stranski has been coercing, blackmailing, and using high ranking government officials, police, and anyone else who can benefit his position.'

Shack looked at Amanda for a second then back to Konni.

The surprised look on Shack's face made the Russian smile. 'It is true my friends . . . He has also supported other more deadly operations in the UK. You will, I'm sure, remember the two very serious incidents involving the poisoning of Sergei Skripal and the more recent unpleasantness in Salisbury.'

'Stranski did that?' said Shack.

'No, not directly, but he supported the operatives who did.'

'Operatives?' said Amanda.

'Russian agents, Miss Amanda. Operatives of the Russian Secret Service. The FSB.'

She put her cup and saucer on the tray. 'So you are saying the Count worked for the FSB?'

Konni shook his head a little. 'As I have already said. He was no Count . . . Oleg Stranski was, before coming to England, a Colonel in the KGB. And in answer to your question, yes, he has worked for the FSB ever since.'

Chapter Forty Four
'Brothers'

The *Angelina* began to gain speed. Shack looked at his watch, almost six-thirty. He looked out of the big window and saw the coastline to starboard. They were heading south.

Konstantine was still on his feet. Still presenting his lecture . . . 'You see, we have been watching you for some time. Ivan here not only saved your life this morning . . . as it is most certain that Stranski would have killed you both and you would now be lying in the tomb he currently occupies.'

Ivan nodded. 'This is true . . . For sure you would not be here now, my friends.'

Konni continued. 'We also saved your life on Hammersmith Bridge. The woman Sokolova was one of Stranski's latest, and I have to say unwilling, assets. The girl's parents were visited by an agent in the Ukraine. Both were, shall we say, rather badly beaten. Pictures of which were sent to their daughter in London, with the assurance they would be tortured and murdered if she did not do as Stranski wanted . . . kill you both.'

'So it was your man who shot her on the bridge?'

Konni shook his head. 'Not my man . . . My girl.' He nodded to the woman standing out on deck. 'You remember Tonya?'

Shack turned. 'Yes, I remember her.'

'Well, she has been looking after you for several days now. In fact she has been a key player in this whole affair.'

Shack frowned and adjusted his eye-patch. 'Key player?'

'Stranski thought he had an undercover asset in our organisation.'

'Tonya,' said Amanda.

'Yes . . . But I'm afraid he was not as smart as he thought. Tonya, as you see, does indeed work for us.'

'So you knew his every move?'

'Not quite every move. But when you came aboard in London, with the bugs he had planted in Amanda's apartment . . . The bugs you thought we had placed . . .'

'Er yeah . . . sorry about that.'

Konni raised his hand in a forgiving gesture then sat down beside Ivan. 'We knew then it was time to increase our surveillance of him . . . and of course . . . you two.'

Amanda gave a little laugh. 'So you are saying you have been looking after us?'

The Russians nodded.

Shack raised his hand. 'Just hold on a minute. I've a couple of questions.'

'Please, go ahead.'

'How did you know where we would be this morning? And how were you there at the precise time? And if you knew all along where that was,' he pointed to the big trunk, 'why were you so intent on getting Irina Seranova's diary? Why not just go get it for yourself?'

Konstantin leaned forward. 'I see why you are such a good detective, Shack. You ask all the right questions.'

Shack grinned at the flattery. 'Yeah, right.'

'How did we know where you were? We knew Stranski was following you. And had you under surveillance for some time. When you left London and headed north, he of course followed.'

Amanda interrupted. 'So you put a tracker in my car.'

Konni shook his head. 'No. We put the tracker in Stranski's Bentley.'

'Hold on a second,' said Shack, 'I can understand if you were following us, Stranski and us, by road. But, and I'm sure this little tub can do a rate of knots, but there's no way you could have kept pace with us at sea.'

'Very true. Angelina can make almost forty knots. But you are correct, we could not keep pace with you. That is why we sailed north yesterday.'

'No, no, no, that's not right. We left London early morning. It was late afternoon when we got up here. If you were planning on helping us you must have known the final destination. You must have known we would ultimately be going to Whitby.'

Konni smiled. 'We did.'

Shack sighed. 'Okay, so if you did know, then why all this anarchy over the diary? Why not just come and get that,' again he pointed to the trunk, 'yourself?'

'Because we did not know where it was. We knew it was somewhere in the town, but not exactly where. And as you had the diary and Volodin's journal, you and the lovely Miss Amanda here were the only ones who could find it.'

'Just a second,' said Amanda. 'I get it you had no idea of the exact location, but how did you know to go to Whitby in the first place?'

Konni turned to Ivan. 'Maybe you should explain, brother?'

This time Ivan stood up, assuming the role of lecturer. 'Da, brother.' He waited for a second or two as if thinking . . . then began. 'You had Irina Seranova's diary. Her mother's diary I should say.'

Amanda nodded.

'And Captain Volodin's journal.'

Again she nodded.

'And of course with these two books you are able to discover several things. I think your Russian is good, Da?'

'It isn't perfect, but I managed to translate and understand the documents.'

Ivan frowned. 'Documents?'

'Sorry, I mean the diary and the journal.'

'Ah, okay.'

'Davai, brother,' said Konstantin. 'Get to the story.'

Ivan raised his hand apologetically. 'Da, okay, okay. So we know the five *children*. The Tsar's five treasure chests were taken from Moscow by Volodin. And we know from Moscow he travels to Saint Petersburg. Then by ship to England.'

'We know all this,' said Shack.

Again the Russian frowned. 'Patience, Mister Shack, patience.'

'Sorry.'

Ivan went over to the big trunk. His footsteps made a crackling sound as he walked over the tarpaulin. He took hold of one of the handles and lifted. He got the end of the trunk off the floor then lowered it again. 'Is very heavy, da?'

Shack nodded and mimicked the big Russian. 'Da, is very heavy.'

The Russian smiled at the gesture, then returned to the group. 'You think Volodin could move five of those,' he pointed at the chest, 'alone?'

No one said anything. Konstantin smiled.

'Captain Volodin had a trusted friend with him. Another officer from the Imperial Guard.' He paused for obvious effect . . . 'Lieutenant Grigory Permyak . . . My grandfather.'

'Your grandfather!' said Amanda.' There is no mention of anyone called Grigory Permyak in Volodin's journal.'

Shack had his phone out, scrolling through the transcript . . . 'Just a second. Listen . . .
We journeyed as Demeter did till claw-like rocks she found . . . Blah blah blah.'

Amanda nodded. 'Right . . . We! We journeyed. Volodin was not alone.'

Ivan smiled. 'Not alone. With my grandfather. And from my grandfather to my father to me, we are told they arrived to England in the place called Whitby.'

Konni stood and put his arm around Ivan's shoulders. 'So this is how we know where to go.'

Shack leaned forward again. 'But if you knew about Whitby from your grandfather, why didn't he tell you, or your father, where that was hidden?'

Ivan looked at him. 'Because he had sworn sacred oath to Volodin. They were as brothers. He would never break oath. Not to brother.'

With his arm still round Ivan's shoulders, Konni said, 'Never . . . Not to a brother.'

For a second, Shack envied the obvious friendship between these two hard men.

Chapter Forty Five
'The Duchess'

They'd been sailing for well over an hour. More tea and coffee had been brought in and the steward had advised the breakfast buffet was now laid in the upper saloon.

Shack pointed to the trunk. 'So, are you planning on opening that any time soon?'

The question had barely passed his lips when Konni and Ivan suddenly stood up, almost to attention.

'Good morning, everyone.'

Amanda and Shack turned and looked at the old lady. They both stood up. Amanda recognised the Gucci slacks and loafers. The Channel jacket over the plain silk shirt finished off the ensemble.

That's one stylish lady, thought Amanda..

Konni went over and kissed her hand. 'Good morning.' He held her arm and escorted her into the saloon.

Ivan quickly moved a comfortable chair for her. 'Good morning.'

As she sat down she smiled and touched his hand. 'Thank you, my dear.' She took a deep breath . . . 'Now . . . who are these lovely people?'

Ivan stepped back as Konstantin made the introductions. 'These are the friends we spoke of. This is Amanda Lang and Shackleton Blister.'

The woman's eyes twinkled like pale sapphires; her gentle smile lit up her face. 'And I am very pleased to meet you both at last.'

Konni waited until she'd finished speaking. 'And this is Her Highness the Duchess Anastasia Marina Seranova. Granddaughter of the late Tsar Nicholas the second. And true heir to the throne of Russia.'

For several seconds Shack and Amanda stood in silence The shocked look on their faces made the Duchess smile . . . 'But please, you must call me Anna.'

Everyone resumed their seats. 'You are, Anna Seranova?' said Amanda.

'Yes, my dear.'

'Irina's daughter?'

The old lady nodded. 'The very same.'

'Then I'm sorry about your mother. Please accept my condolences. I knew her . . . unhappily not for long. She was an amazing lady.'

'Excuse me, Duchess,' said Shack.

'Anna, please . . . Anna.'

'Yes of course, Anna. And I mean this with the utmost respect, but you don't look old enough to be the granddaughter of . . . well . . . the Tsar!'

The gentle smile appeared. 'My dear, Shackleton. I can assure you I am. I shall be celebrating my seventy-fifth birthday in a couple of months.'

'But, but you don't even look sixty!'

His blurted out compliment was accepted graciously. 'You are very gallant.'

Amanda shot him a disapproving glance. 'But often speaks before thinking.'

'That's quite alright.'

Shack raised his hand slightly. 'So it was these guys who took you from your place at *Luton Hoo* a few days ago?'

'Yes. They were aware Stranski had discovered my location. Hence their swift action.'

'Right. So you left in the morning and Stranski showed up in the afternoon . . . According to the old guy at your place.'

'Gavin, Major Gavin Trench. He's such a dear. Yes, that's correct.'

'I'm sorry to go on, Duchess . . . Anna. But with respect. I don't get all this ?' He waved his hand between her and the Russians. 'These guys are protecting you?' He turned to Konni. 'No offence, by the way.'

'None taken,' said Konni.

The Duchess leaned forward. 'I'm not sure what you mean, Shackleton?'

Shack frowned. 'Not sure how delicately I can say this . . .'

Seeing his hesitation, Amanda said, 'Russian Mafia?'

The Duchess and the Russians all laughed.

Konni looked at Shack. 'You think we are Mafia?'

Shack said nothing for several seconds . . . 'So you're not?'

Konni looked at Ivan. The men grinned, then Ivan said, 'We are not completely legal, although we do have much legitimate business. We are not into drugs or trafficking, but we are very skilled at smuggling and we . . .'

Konni put his hand on Ivan's arm. 'I think that is enough information, brother.' He turned to Shack. 'We may be villains, Mister Shack, but we are not bad men. Although from time to time we must do bad things. What we are, as I believe I told you when we first met, are loyal Romanovia.'

175

'Queen Elizabeth the first,' said Anna, 'had her Privateers . . . Essentially pirates, loyal to the Crown. There is a parallel here, my dear Shackleton.'

Shack grinned. 'Pirates and Privateers . . . Ain't that the truth.'

Konni stood up and spoke to the Duchess. 'Can we get you anything before we begin?'

'No thank you. I had tea in my stateroom.' She looked at the trunk.' Now I'm rather excited to see what's inside.'

Konni nodded, then Ivan stood and went out on deck, returning with the bolt-cutter guy.

The Duchess held out her arm. 'A moment please.' Konni helped her to her feet. 'Let me see the chest.' He assisted her across the cracking tarpaulin. 'Could I have a napkin please?'

Shack took one from the tray and handed it to her. She bent down and slowly wiped the dust from the top of the trunk, then stood back. A tear rolled down her cheek. Written in elegant Cyrillic was one name, *ANASTASIA*. She touched the hard, cracked sealing wax on the locks and gently ran a finger across the Romanoff eagle. No one spoke. It was clear this was a special moment for her.

She took a small handkerchief from her pocket and held it to her cheek. 'Oh, dear. Now I'm just being a sentimental old woman.'

Konni took her arm and helped her back to her chair. 'Are you okay?'

'I'm fine, my dear. Thank you.'

Ivan looked at the Duchess. 'Shall we begin?'

She nodded.

Chapter Forty Six
'The Inventory'

The muscles in the man's arm bulged as he strained against the bolt-cutters. The snap of broken metal made Anna flinch as the jaws cut through the ancient lock. It fell to the tarpaulin with a clunk, the hundred year old sealing wax disintegrating into several pieces. The man moved to the second lock and began again. He mumbled something in Russian as he strained against the thick steel. Ivan grinned. The metal snapped leaving the lock hanging in the hasp. The big guy unhooked it, picked up the other and brushed the remains of the seals to one side.

With a wave of his hand and a, 'Spasiba,' Ivan dismissed him.

For several seconds they all looked at the chest. Ivan turned to the Duchess. She nodded.

The old hinges creaked as the top was eased open. Ivan let it fall back against the robust leather support-straps. Everyone, except the Duchess, stood to get a better view. No one spoke.

The interior was divided into two halves. Each half was filled to capacity with what appeared to be silken bags of various sizes. Every bag was secured with a draw string and appeared to have a simple luggage label attached. In the lid was a slotted cavity which held a couple of ledgers. Ivan turned to Anna, then removed the books from the lid. He opened one. 'These look like account books. All in English.' He turned and handed one to Anna, the other to Konstantin.

The Duchess carefully opened the ledger. 'This is the inventory.'

Konni nodded. 'Da.'

Ivan picked up a smallish pouch and looked at the label. 'Number one-hundred and seven.'

Konni and Anna began going through the pages. A few moments later Konni said, 'Here we are. One-hundred and seven. Three cabochon emeralds. Five, eight and eleven carats.'

Ivan took the bag to the table and carefully emptied the contents. Three items, each wrapped in tissue paper fell out. Konni picked one up and removed the wrapping. He held the stone up to the light, then smiled as the sun sparkled through the magnificent jewel.

He handed the stone to Anna, then read from the ledger again. 'Gifted to the Tsarina by the Sultan of Morocco. Value, two-thousand eight hundred pounds.'

'Not bad,' said Shack.

Ivan was tapping away on his smartphone. 'But that was 1919 . . . today's value is . . . over one-hundred and forty thousand pounds.'

'How many bags are there?' asked Amanda.

Anna turned the pages, 'This begins at one, and ends at a sixty-five.'

Konni held up his ledger. 'This is sixty-six to one-hundred and ten.'

'Over a hundred bags,' said Shack. 'And if that one is anything to go by, there's a king's ransom in there.'

'A Tsar's ransom, my dear Shackleton. That's why the inventory is in English. The *five children*, the five chest were to pay the British government to grant the Tsar and his family sanctuary.'

Shack turned and looked at the open chest. 'Sorry to sound crass. But is there a total value?'

'This one says two and a half million,' said Konstantin.

The Duchess turned to the final page. 'And this is almost three and a half million.'

A few seconds passed as Ivan calculated the current value. He looked up and smiled, then turned the phone for all to see. 'Almost three-hundred million pounds.'

For what seemed an age no one spoke. The only sound was the hum of the powerful diesel engines as the *Angelina* sailed south.

'I think we should have Mister Steinman take over,' said the Duchess.

Konni nodded and went to the house-phone. 'Da. Please ask Steinman to join us.'

A short while later a very dapper older gentlemen entered. He bowed his head slightly. 'Good morning, madam.' His English diction was perfect, but the accent was heavy Russian.

The old lady smiled. 'Good morning, Avi.'

'Avi,' said Konstantin, 'I think we have rather a big job for you this time old friend.' He handed the inventories to Steinman. 'I think we first need to confirm what is in these, is actually in there.' He pointed to the chest.

The old man put on his spectacles and opened the first ledger. All eyes were on him as he studied the pages. A couple of minutes later he closed the book and looked over his glasses. 'A big job. Yes indeed, a very big job.'

Konstantin put his hand on Avi's shoulder 'Okay, old friend. We will leave you to make a start.' He turned to the others. 'And I think we should all go and have breakfast.'

Chapter Forty Seven
'Breakfast at Tiffany's'

The upper-deck saloon was only slightly smaller than the lower. In the centre an elegantly laid dining table had been set. Along one side of the saloon a bank of serving dishes held a variety of hot food. Fruits, breads and danish, along with a dripping honeycomb, were on a separate table. Fruit juice in crystal jugs sparkled in the sunlight. An ornate silver wine cooler held three bottles of champagne and a large bottle of vodka.

'Eat your heart out, Ritz Hotel,' said Shack.

'I hope you are hungry,' said Konni.

As they helped themselves to food the steward appeared with fresh pots of tea and coffee. With plates loaded, they all took their seats.

'This is not what I was expecting when we got bundled into Amanda's car this morning, Ivan.'

The Russian narrowed his eyes and chuckled. 'Da. Maybe you think is over, eh tough guy?'

The look on Shack's face said it all. 'I was a bit concerned, yeah.'

They all laughed.

After breakfast, Konni stood up. 'Please excuse me. I'll be back shortly.' On his way out he touched Anna on the shoulder. She nodded. Clearly she knew why he left.

Amanda caught the gesture. 'Everything alright?'

'Yes, my dear. Actually Konstantin is arranging something for you.'

'Oh, really?'

The old lady patted Amanda's hand. 'A little something for your help.'

'Now I'm intrigued,'

Anna kept hold of Amanda's hand. 'There is something I would like you to do for me, my dear.'

'If I can.'

'My mother's diary and father's journal. Once you have finished with them, I would really like to have them.'

'Yes, yes of course. You must have them. This all started with the writing of Irina's . . . your mother's memoir. So I'd like to finish that if I may?'

'Certainly, you must. And once it's finished I shall be the first to read it.'

Amanda smiled. 'May I ask a question?'

'Yes'

'Irina told me she had no family. Why would she say that?'

The Duchess sat back in her chair and clasped her hands together.

Amanda sensed the body-language. 'I'm sorry . . . If it's a painful or private matter, please forget I asked.'

Anna leaned forward. 'No . . . I'm fine, my dear. I'm fine, Yes it is painful but not in the way you think. It was painful because we could not be together. You see, I am the last in the blood-line and my mother, your friend Irina, wanted to protect me. It was not safe for either of us to be together. So we lived apart. We did communicate of course. Phone calls and now in this day and age we have all kinds of video links, which made it a little more bearable. And once or twice a year we would arrange to meet somewhere.'

'That is so sad you could not spend your lives together. Even when she died you . . . ' The old lady's eyes began to fill-up. 'Oh, I'm sorry.'

Anna took out her handkerchief again. 'I knew today was going to be sad . . . So let's brighten it a little.' The Duchess smiled. 'Tell me about your time with my mother?'

On the other side of the saloon Shack was in conversation with Ivan. They were standing at the breakfast buffet when Konstantin returned.

Konni put his hand on the Duchess's shoulder. 'Excuse me, Miss Amanda,' then leaned down close to the old lady. 'It's done.'

Anna smiled and touched his hand.

The Russian joined the men. 'Now, what are you guys up to?'

'Ivan here was telling me a bit more about the late Count Stranski,' said Shack.

Konstantin nodded then picked up a bottle of Krug. As the cork popped the ladies turned. He held up the bottle. 'Anna?'

'With a little juice please.'

'Miss Amanda?'

'Same for me, thank you.'

After serving the ladies' drinks he said to Shack, 'You want some of this?'

Shack frowned and nodded to the bottle of vodka. 'Rather have a shot of that.'

Ivan and Konni smiled.

It was almost midday when the Duchess, Shack and Amanda, and the Russians returned to the lower saloon. Avi Steinman had been busy. The trunk was now empty, its contents spread out along the banquette seating either side of the saloon. The old Jew was busy making notes on a pad, oblivious to their arrival.

'How are you doing, Avi?' said Konstantin.

The old man turned. 'Oh, I'm sorry. Excuse me.'

'It's okay. So what do we have, old friend?'

Steinman put his notebook aside and picked up the ledgers. 'As you see, I have taken everything from the chest. And I can confirm each numbered bag is indeed recorded in this inventory, all one-hundred and ten bags.' He pointed to the bar area. 'And I have taken a random selection of ten of the larger bags to verify their contents.'

They all turned toward the bar.

'Oh, my God!' said Amanda.

'It's *Breakfast at Tiffany's*,' said Shack.

The whole bar-top was covered with the most amazing array of jewellery. Tiaras, bracelets, necklaces. Fabulous pieces of artwork encrusted with sparkling gems of every colour.

'I'm sorry, Konstantin, but it is going to take me several weeks to verify each and every item in the inventory.'

The big Russian didn't turn. His eyes were still transfixed on the unbelievable array in front of them. 'Don't worry, Avi . . . You shall have all the time you need in Italy.'

Chapter Forty Eight
'The Contessa'

Ivan excused himself, then returned a short while later with two of his guys. Each man had a large, sturdy aluminium suitcase on wheels.

'Avi,' he said, 'pack everything into these.' He turned to his men and pointed to the old trunk, 'Get rid of that.'

'Wait,' said the Duchess, 'I would really like to keep the chest.'

Ivan nodded. 'Of course, yes of course.' Then again to his men. 'Get someone to clean that up.'

The two guys closed up the big trunk and carried it away.

The old lady smiled. 'Thank you, my dear. I also think we should make the call to the Contessa before Mister Steinman repacks everything?'

Konni went to the bar and picked up the house phone. 'Captain, put a satellite call through to Florence. Bring it up on the saloon screen, please . . . Da . . . Da . . . Thank you, Rustam.'

Anna took a seat facing the big TV screen. Konstantin switched on the set.

'The Contessa?' said Shack to no one in particular.

'Friends in Italy,' said Ivan.

'Old friends in Italy,' said Anna.

The *Facetime* logo filled the TV screen. A few seconds later a very elegant lady appeared. She was seated in front of a large bookcase, which looked to be filled with fine leather-bound volumes. 'Buongiorno.'

Anna raised her hand. 'Buongiorno, Maria. How are you?'

'Hello, Anna. Yes, we are all well. I see you are still onboard?'

'We are, and I'm looking forward to being with you again.'

'When do you plan to arrive?'

Konni raised his hand. 'Hello, Contessa.'

'Konstantin. Hello.'

'We'll be in Monaco for about a week, then sail for Livorno before the end of the month.'

'Wonderful, wonderful . . . I see Ivan there . . . Hello, darling.'

Ivan waved. 'Contessa. Is always good to see you.'

'Are you behaving yourself, cara mia?'

The big Russian grinned. 'Sometimes I think.'

The Countess chuckled. 'And who else do we have there?'

'You will remember our old friend Mister Steinman,' said Konni.

'Ah yes, I do indeed, shalom.'

The old man waved.

'And these are our new friends . . . Miss Amanda Lang and Mister Shackleton Blister. This is The Contessa Maria Alaria di Vincenzo. A very special friend of ours.'

'Ah, yes, Lady Amanda, I know your father, Lord Lang.'

'Hello, Contessa.'

'And the dashing, Shackleton Blister. A formidable asset I am told.'

Shack smiled and adjusted the eye-patch. 'Not sure about that, Contessa.'

The Contessa put on spectacles. 'And I see you have found *Anastasia.*'

Konni stepped to one side. 'We have, and it is more than we expected.' He picked up a beautiful sapphire and diamond necklace. 'We have only opened a few of the items, but as you see, Contessa, they are all magnificent.'

The woman nodded. 'A great contribution to the cause. Well done all of you. I'll let you get on.'

'I'll give you a call later, Maria,' said Anna, 'there are a couple of things I need to talk about.'

Again the Contessa nodded. 'Very well. Until later then.' She raised her hand, 'Goodbye for now, *ciao tutti.*' The screen went blank.

Shack went over to the bar and picked up a bejewelled tiara. 'I have to say I'm feelin a bit outa place now.'

'Why so?' said Anna.

He held up the tiara. 'All this stuff . . . the Russian heavy mob,' he turned to Konni, 'no offence by the way. Lady Amanda, Duchess Anastasia, The Contessa di whatsit . . . then there's little old me.'

No one spoke for several seconds . . . then they all laughed.

Chapter Forty Nine
'The Secret'

The group had decamped to the rear sun deck to allow Avi Steinman to repack the treasure. Outside on deck there was another smaller bar, with a steward in attendance. Once seated the steward served drinks. Amanda and the Duchess soon fell into deep conversation, clearly getting along. The Russians drank beer and vodka chasers, Shack stuck to beer.

The absence of any minders was noticeable. Shack smiled, ever so slightly, *Part of the team now,* he thought to himself.

Konstantin caught the smile. 'So, Mister Shack, why you smile?'

'Like I said earlier, this is all a little surreal for an ordinary bloke like me.'

'I think you are not that ordinary, tough-guy,' said Ivan.

Shack touched the eye-patch. 'You mean this?' He held up his scarred hands. 'Or these?'

The Russians were silent for a few seconds, then Konni said, 'We know your story, my friend. You were a policeman . . . An honest policeman. And for this you lost your wife and were sent to prison. But you are here now, and you have survived.'

Shack looked towards the coastline, a few miles to starboard. 'Maybe.'

Ivan leaned forward and clinked glasses. '*Nostrovia mia drugg.*'

'Amanda's the one who speaks Russian mate, not me.'

Konni leaned forward and touched glasses. 'Ivan says, *Cheers my friend.*'

'Ah, okay . . . cheers. So, guys, what's the plan for us? You gonna dock in London?'

Konstantin shook his head. 'We need to get to Monaco. We will rendezvous with a launch out of Southend. Captain Rustam has arranged for a transfer for you. There will also be a chauffeur car waiting on the dock.'

'Okay, sounds good, what's our ETA?'

'Early evening. Seven o'clock, maybe a little later.'

Shack looked at his watch, then held up his glass. 'Great. Time for a few more then.'

Konstantin laughed, then waved the steward over.

Amanda and the Duchess both declined the offer of more wine.

'One or two glasses is enough for me these days I'm afraid,' said the old lady.

'I drink a little more than I should,' Amanda nodded towards Shack, 'I blame him.'

The Duchess laughed.

'May I ask a couple of questions, Anna?'

'Of course, my dear.'

'Who is the Contessa and what is the cause she spoke of?'

'Ah . . . the ever enquiring journalist comes out.'

'If it's . . .'

'No it's perfectly fine, my dear. And only fair you should know, after what you have done to help us.'

'She said she knew my father, but I don't ever recall him mentioning her.'

'Maria Alaria . . . the Contessa, is an old friend and is the current head of one of the most powerful organisations in the world . . . *The Templari Incrementum.*'

Amanda frowned, then took a sip of wine. 'I always thought they were just a legend . . . like the *Illuminati.*'

'How is your Latin?'

'Not good I'm afraid, but I do know that the *Templari* are supposed to be the descendants of the *Knights Templars.*'

'Exactly so, my dear, and believe me, they are certainly not just a legend.'

'That's quite a revelation . . . and now they support the Romanovia.'

'Not now, always . . . You see the death of the Tsar gave birth to the Romanovia. Loyal Russians, thousands across the world, who wish to see a Romanov back on the throne.'

'I see, and that's the cause the Contessa spoke of, and the treasure will help fund that.'

'There are many who contribute . . . We have, as I've already said, loyal friends around the world who support us, even within Mother Russia.'

'So this is the big secret Irina, your mother, spoke of?'

'Perhaps, but I think she was referring to something less noble. Something I believe you, and your wonderful friend over there, have already discovered.'

'We have?'

'Volodin's journal has all the answers . . . if you are able to read between the lines. You visited the Archives at Westminster?'

'Yes, but not everything was available to us.'

The old lady smiled. 'And there you have it, my dear. That, I believe, is the secret Irina spoke of.'

'But what we found was common knowledge. The Tsar coming to England. Of his request for sanctuary from the Bolsheviks.'

'Yes, this is history. But what really happened is not.'

Amanda raised her glass to the steward. 'I think I need another drink.'

The steward poured her wine then offered more to the Duchess. She shook her head.

Amanda took a sip. 'So what don't we know?'

The old lady sighed deeply. 'The Tsar and his family were indeed promised a home in England and the *five children*, the *five chests* were to pay the British for allowing this . . . Well, four were to pay the British, the fifth, *Anastasia,* was to be held back and would be used to fund the fight to regain the throne.'

'Ah, I see.'

'But there were elements in the government who didn't want to support the Tsar in case it spawned a similar revolution in England.'

'Yes, I know that. Not the most charitable of decisions on our part.'

'But they'd already been paid and were in possession of four chest filled with the same kind of treasure as we have in there.'

'A Tsar's ransom.'

The Duchess nodded. 'Yes, a Tsar's ransom. If they didn't want him in England, they could have easily helped to get the family to America or Canada. Especially with the vast wealth in the chests.'

Amanda nodded. 'Yes, yes . . . I've wondered why something like that never happened.'

The old lady sighed again. 'It never happened because the British Government waited.' She brushed a tear from her cheek. 'They waited until he and his family were arrested and murdered . . . And they kept the treasure.'

Chapter Fifty
'Ublyudok'

The rest of the trip was spent enjoying the short voyage to the Thames Estuary. A rather splendid lunch had been laid out in the upper saloon, which not only fed the group, but whiled away another three hours. Konstantin frequently excused himself to make various 'calls' but Ivan remained as the genial host. Something Shack found slightly bizarre, considering he, Ivan, had left a dead body in the Whitby graveyard. A thought that prompted a few questions to the Russian . . .

They were out on deck when Shack asked, 'So, my fine Russian friend, what's going to happen to Stranski?'

Ivan grinned. 'Direct as ever, Mister Shack.'

'It's pretty obvious you intend him to be found, otherwise why leave a flash-drive on the body?'

The Russian leaned on the rail and watched the big wind-turbines a few miles to port. 'The flash-stick has much evidence.'

'I would image that, but what?'

'Stranski, as we said this morning was FSB. The evidence will expose many people involved with this . . . *ublyudok.*'

Shack smiled. He didn't know what the word meant but certainly got the intonation. 'Okay, I get it. All you do is let the cops know where the body is and *bosh* . . . Stranski's network is history.'

'Bosh?'

193

Shack waved his hand. 'Means, hey-presto . . . like magic.'

'Da . . . Like magic. I like this word . . . *Bosh.*'

They both laughed.

Konstantin joined them. 'A joke?'

Shack shook his head, 'No, mate. Just my vocabulary.'

'Okay, Mister Shack. We will be at the rendezvous in an hour. I think we join the ladies and have a parting drink.'

'Sounds good to me, mate.'

'Da,' said Ivan, '*bosh.*'

Konstantin looked at his friend. 'What?'

'Don't worry,' said Shack. 'That's me teaching him English.'

This time Konni laughed.

The *Angelina* began to reduce speed as the Essex coastline came into view. The group had assembled on the rear deck along with a couple of minders and deck-crew. Shack saw Tonya arrive with a small holdall.

Konstantin said, 'Tonya has said she will go with you and see you safely home.'

'There's really no need,' said Amanda.

'There is also a little business with a Bentley to deal with.'

Shack grinned. 'You got a buyer for Stranski's car already, Konni?'

The Russian winked, then turned to Amanda. 'I think I would feel better, Miss Amanda. Please allow me to do this last kindness?'

'Sure, why not?'

'Or you could come with me to Monaco?'

'Hmm . . . now there's an offer a girl doesn't get every day.'

'Well?'

'I don't think so . . . But thank you, Konstantin. The last few days have been exciting enough.'

'I'll come!'

The Russian laughed. 'Okay, Mister Shack, you are welcome also.'

'Just kidding, mate. Like the boss said . . . We need to go home.'

Chapter Fifty One
'Dasvidanya'

They watched as the young pilot manoeuvred the motor-launch skilfully up to Angelina's rear landing-deck. Captain Rustam held the super-yacht steady against the prevailing current. The two deckhands hooked onto the launch, then secured it bow and stern with light ropes.

Tonya gave a quick nod to Konni then went down to the landing-deck. Shack watched as three men disembarked the launch, then realised it was the guys Ivan had tasked with driving off the Bentley, Amanda's car, and the old van in Whitby.

The three greeted Tonya as she went aboard the launch, one in a more friendly manner than the others. The three trotted up the steps and greeted Konstantin and Ivan. One spoke quietly to Ivan. Nods and fist bumps were exchanged.

Ivan turned to Amanda. 'Your car is at home. Valeted and tank filled. Concierge has key.'

Shack chuckled. 'Valeted and topped up. Nice touch, mate.'

Konni shook hands with Shack. '*Dasvidanya*, my friend. I hope we meet again.'

'Who knows, maybe we will. But perhaps with a little less excitement eh?'

'Yes, less excitement I think.'

Shack winked. 'Thanks, Konni. Take care, eh.'

The smiling Russian took Amanda's hand and kissed it. 'You are sure you would not like to come to Monaco, Miss Amanda?'

She smiled. 'Thank you, Konstantin. Maybe another time.'

Ivan also kissed her hand. '*Dasvidanya*, beautiful lady.'

Finally they turned to Anna. 'Goodbye, Duchess,' said Shack. 'I hope you have a safe and happy life.'

Amanda kissed the old lady's cheek. 'Goodbye, Anna, it's been an honour to meet you.'

Anna took her hand and looked into Amanda's eyes. 'Goodbye, my dear. God bless you.'

They went down to the landing-deck. Tonya and one of the deck-hands helped them aboard.

As the ropes were untied Ivan called down. 'Hey, tough guy.'

Shack looked up.

'It's been emotional.'

Shack laughed.

The launch eased away from *Angelina's* stern, then increased speed to the mouth of the Thames. Shack and Amanda waved to the small party on the rear deck.

'I think that's enough excitement for a while. What d'you think, Y'Ladyship?'

She linked her arm through his. 'Ain't that the truth.'

He laughed at the use of his catchphrase. 'Sure is, luv.'

They continued to watch as the super-yacht slowly picked up speed.

Amanda sighed. 'To think, I could have been in Monaco in a few of days.'

The force of the blast-wave almost knocked them off their feet. From bow to stern the hull and superstructure were torn to pieces by simultaneous explosions. In less than a second the multimillion pound super-yacht had turned into a massive ball of fire.

For several seconds they watched, transfixed and in shock at what just happened. The *Angelina*, now no more than a huge blazing inferno began to sink. The pall of oil-black smoke, like some hideous genie of death, floated a hundred feet into the evening sky.

The launch's young pilot eased back on the throttle and began to change course to look for survivors.

'Do not go back. Keep straight ahead.' shouted Tonya.

Shack and Amanda turned to see the Russian pointing a small Walther automatic at them. In the other hand she held her smartphone.

'Take it easy you two.'

The launch began to slow. She yelled again. 'I said straight ahead . . . Do as I say, or you will get this,' she held up the gun for the young lad to see.

The boat increased speed.

Tonya looked at her two captives, she shook her head slightly. 'You British . . . You have no idea what is going on around you. You are more stupid than them.' She waved the smartphone towards the blazing hull of the sinking *Angelina*.

Shack moved closer to Amanda. He slipped an arm around her waist. Then pointed to the stricken vessel. 'You did this.'

The Russian's eyes narrowed. She held up her phone. 'With one touch and . . . boom!'

'So you were really working with Stranski all the time,' said Amanda.

'All the time. And these stupid Romanovia think I am theirs.'

'And us?' said Shack.

She slipped the phone in her pocket then cocked the Walther. The launch slowed again.

'I said go straight.' She turned slightly and waved the gun at the boatman.

In that instant Shack lunged. The crack of the gun-shot echoed across the cold water of the Thames as he and the Russian went over the side.

For what seemed an age the launch covered the area. The motor gurgling slowly as it circled the place Shack and Tonya had gone in. Several other small boats were heading out towards the slowly sinking *Angelina* . . . then . . .

'Ahhgggg . . .' Shack broke water a few feet from the side of the launch.

The eye-patch had gone. A large gash on his forehead oozed blood. In a couple of strokes he was alongside and being pulled aboard by the shocked and scared young boatman.

'Amanda? . . . Amanda, is she okay?' He coughed and spluttered, gasping for breath as he tumbled onto the deck. 'Is she okay?'

The young lad slowly shook his head. 'She's dead.'

Chapter Fifty Two
3 Days Later

'That is one hell of a story,' said Detective Chief Inspector Reynolds.

'So what happens next?' said Shack.

'I know this is a very difficult time for you, so your help is really appreciated. And for now, as far as you are concerned, I think we're done. You've provided us with excellent information, plus the location of the body in Whitby. The evidence on the flash-drive is going to cause one hell of a stink. . . . No pun intended.'

Shack smiled.

'Special Branch and Five are going to be well pissed-off. The fact that Oleg Stranski was able to operate a network, for decades, without them knowing is going to be embarrassing to say the least. Especially so, considering his involvement with the Salisbury poisonings.'

'Okay, good. And I guess you'll pass on the evidence to Devon police regarding the murder of Julie Lawson?'

'Oh, no. We'll take that case ourselves. We're not having the woodentops down there stomping all over it in their size twelves. It's all linked to Stranski anyway, so it's definitely our case.'

'And the Thomson woman at *Seaview Downs*?'

'She'll be charged with conspiracy to murder, and embezzlement. Her days of helping herself to the home's funds are over.'

Shack nodded. 'That flash-drive is certainly going to boost your clear-up rate. Maxine Arnold and her husband, Julie Lawson, not to mention Irina Seranova.'

'Very true . . . It's fair to say Stranski didn't actually carry out any of the killings, but he certainly had his people do them.'

Shack stood up and they shook hands. 'Looks like your Deputy Chief Constable bid is in the bag then.'

Reynold's eyes narrowed, then he smiled. 'Let's just say it's not going to do it any harm.'

'Right, thanks, Chief Inspector. Let me know if I can be of any further help.'

'Thank you again, sir. And I'm really sorry about Miss Lang.'

* * *

The carpark was full so Shack left Amanda's Evoque on a side street. It was a short walk back, but the air would do him good. The stiches in the gash on his forehead were itching, but he resisted the urge to scratch. His meeting with Reynolds and the reliving of the last few days had been challenging, especially the shooting of Amanda.

He stepped out onto the road. The cyclist swerved and yelled. 'Look where you're going you idiot!'

He watched as the irate Lycra-clad figure sped away, then looked both ways and crossed the road. Once inside, the familiar smell assaulted his nostrils. He inadvertently rubbed his nose causing a sneeze. The place was just as busy as the last time he was here. He continued along the corridor until he saw the discreet sign, MORTUARY. A woman came out, dressed in green scrubs, and nodded. He turned left and continued on.

The windows in this corridor were open and the fresh morning air a welcome relief. A couple of staff members obviously recognised the man with the eye-patch and smiled.

At the door he stood for a second, then said. 'Good morning Y'Ladyship.'

She turned and smiled. 'Hey. Good morning.'

He moved to the other side of the bed, took hold of her hand, then bent down and kissed her forehead. 'How are you feeling?'

'Not sure really . . . They have me on this.' She held up a small clicker-like gadget that was attached to a machine. 'If the pain gets too bad I can self-administer. It's lovely.'

He smiled and brushed a lock of hair from her forehead. 'That's good, luv, but don't get to like it too much, eh?' Her hair was secured with a headband and her skin uncharacteristically pale. The dark shadows below her eyes were an indication of what she'd been through. 'I'm glad to see you looking so well.'

'You are such a fibber sometimes.'

He pulled a chair closer to the bed and sat down. He took her hand again. 'The doc says the chunk of liver they cut out would grow back. How cool is that?'

She tried to smile, but it turned into a grimace. She hit the morphine button and the pained look disappeared. She took a deep breath. 'So what have you been up to, darling?'

'Had another meeting with DCI Reynolds earlier.'

'And how is your favourite policeman doing?'

Shack shrugged. 'Yeah right. Have your dad and sister been in today?'

'Yes, you just missed them. They've gone for some lunch.'

'Ah, okay.' He took a brown manilla envelope from his jacket. 'This came registered delivery yesterday afternoon.'

'Open it for me, please.'

Shack ran his finger along the flap and took out the letter. He offered it to her.

'Can you read it, darling?'

For a second or two he looked at the document then began . . .

'Dear Miss Lang.

We have been instructed by one of our clients to establish an international account in your name. There has been an initial deposit of three hundred thousand pounds. The client has asked you to consider this sum as a finder's fee. This, along with the sincere gratitude of the client.

To facilitate access to the account we respectfully request you attend the bank in person, with appropriate identification, at a time convenient to you.

If you have any questions please do not hesitate to contact me. I look forward to meeting you and welcoming you as a valued client.

Yours sincerely,

Henry Montrose.

International Accounts Director.

The Merchant Bank of the Isle of Man.'

Shack put the letter down. 'Well, Y'Ladyship. Looks like it's a trip over to Douglas when you get out of here.'

Amanda frowned. 'I don't understand. How could they have set that up?'

'Money, luv, and a satellite phone call from the *Angelina.*'

She moaned and moved slightly in the bed. Another click on the opiate supply and she relaxed. A nurse came in and checked the machines. 'How are you feeling?'

Amanda smiled.

'Would you like some lunch? It's only soup for you I'm afraid.'

'No thank you.'

The nurse left.

'Have they said when you can go home?'

She shook her head slightly. 'The operation was good, but I'm still on antibiotics and being monitored for infection. So no actual mention of release.'

'Well you're in the best place. Better to be safe, luv. I don't want anything else to happen to you.' He squeezed her hand gently.

'Thank you.'

'You're welcome, Y'Ladyship.'

'No . . . I mean thank you for saving my life.'

'I don't know what I'd have done if I'd lost you, Amanda.'

She squeezed his hand. A tear ran down the side of her face. 'Kiss me.'

He kissed her forehead again. She touched his cheek. 'Kiss me properly.'

He wiped the tear from her face, then gently kissed her lips.

'I love you.'

Chapter Fifty Three
'The Major'

Shack was in no hurry to see Major Gavin Trench. He took his time, staying within the speed-limit and, even though the M1 was busy, he was enjoying the drive. What he wasn't looking forward to was telling the old boy what had happened to his friend Anastasia Seranova. The short time he'd spent with Trench had left an impression. Old school. Loyal and dependable. The British Bulldog. *I'd have liked to have known him in his heyday*, he thought.

It was after three when Shack turned off at Junction 10. A few minutes later he passed through the big ornate gates and entered the beautiful *Luton Hoo* estate.

He dropped his speed to ten miles an hour, the better to enjoy the tree-lined drive. A few golfers were out on the course. As he got nearer, the imposing building came into view. He toyed with the idea of nipping in for a shot of Dutch-courage but carried on past the Golf House and down the hill towards *East Gate*.

As he pulled up to the front of the cottage he saw Trench sitting in the garden. The old boy waved as Shack stepped out.

'Hello, young fella. To what do we owe the pleasure?'

Shack raised his hand. 'Hello again, Major. Sorry to disturb, but d'you think we could have a chat, sir?'

'A chat? Of course . . . come on in, or would you prefer to stay out here?'

'Out here's fine, sir.'

'Can I you get you anything? Tea, coffee? Water?'

'You wouldn't have a beer would you? I know I'm driving but one won't hurt.'

Trench smiled. 'Jolly good. Take a pew. Be right back.'

A few minutes later the old boy arrived with a can of Heineken and a glass. 'There you go.'

Shack poured his drink. 'Cheers.'

The Major raised his glass. 'Good health . . . So, what's so important you drive all the way from London to see me?'

Shack sat up and cleared his throat. 'I have some bad news, sir.'

The old man put his glass down. 'Go on?'

'Did you see the news a few days ago? The ship . . . the yacht, that was destroyed in the Thames Estuary?'

Trench nodded. 'I did . . . awful, awful. Said they couldn't say how many were killed. At least fifteen, some damned journalist said. No survivors. Absolutely dreadful . . . Is that your bad news, my boy?'

Shack swallowed another mouthful of beer. 'No sir. You see I, we, Amanda, and I were on that yacht before the explosion. We'd just disembarked and were on a launch coming ashore.'

'Yes?'

'I'm sorry, Major . . . Anna was on the ship. She's dead, sir.'

The old man was silent for a few seconds . . . 'Anna? Dead? No, I don't think so. You must be mistaken, young fella. Anna called me this morning and said she would be away for a little while but would be in touch.'

'Anna Seranova called you this morning? You are sure it was her?'

'Hundred percent. Definitely Anna . . . You look a little surprised there?'

'Surprised? Yes, I suppose I am.'

'Are you alright? You look as if you've seen a ghost.'

'Maybe I have, Major . . . maybe I have.' Shack stood and finished his beer, then held out his hand, 'I'll leave you in peace, sir. It was good to see you again. And thanks for the drink.'

'You sure you're alright?'

'Yes, yes I'm fine.'

'Okay then, anytime you're ever in the neighbourhood, there's always a beer here for you.'

As Shack drove off he lowered the window and waved. A few seconds later he looked at his reflection in the rear-view mirror, and said, *'Anna called this morning,'* and smiled.

EPILOGUE

An Office Somewhere in Moscow.
The day after Sir Rowland Deveraux was charged.

Katarina Elena Draconova had been waiting for almost twenty minutes. It had been a while since she was in this particular office and it always meant the same thing. The heavy door made a clicking sound as the automatic lock was released. The stern-faced woman behind the desk nodded for Katerina to go through.

The man standing by the window turned as she entered. 'Ah, Draco, we have need of your skills once again.'

'Yes, sir.'

'There is a small business delegation going to the UK this evening. Something to do with post-Brexit trade talks,' he made a dismissive gesture with his hand. 'You will join them.'

'Yes, sir.'

'They will be in London for three days only. This is your mission window.'

Katerina nodded. 'Understood.'

'As usual, the subject and all relevant details will be encrypted and sent to your phone shortly. It is vital the subject is neutralised before any . . . shall we say, embarrassing information, is given to the security services.'

'I understand, sir.'

The man smiled. 'Good . . . Very good. Thank you, my dear. Have a pleasant trip.'

The next day in Fortnum & Mason

The variety of hand-made chocolates and confectionaries was amazing, The smell alone was enough to make your mouth water. Katerina browsed the magnificent display as she waited to be served.

The smartly-dressed assistant finished with her customer, then came across. 'Good morning, madam. Sorry to keep you. How may I help you today?'

'I believe you have some rather wonderful Rum Truffles?'

The young assistant smiled. 'Yes, madam. One of our best sellers. We make them with real Caribbean rum and the chocolate is seventy percent coca. Absolutely delicious.'

'Then they are the ones I'm looking for. I'll have six please.'

'Certainly, madam. They are nine pounds each. Would you like them gift wrapped.'

'No, just a normal box is fine. Thank you.'

In the taxi, Katerina took the box from the F&M carrier and slipped off the lid. She picked up one of the truffles and popped it in her mouth. 'Hmm, so that's what nine pounds tastes like.'

'Sorry, miss did you said something?'

She smiled at the driver. 'Just talking to myself.'

'I do it all the time, miss.'

She put the box on the seat, opened her handbag and took out a tiny bottle with a small dropper attached. She drew some of the bottles contents then, with great care, placed a single drop on each truffle.

That afternoon in Pentonville Prison

The overpowering smell of disinfectant failed to mask the underlying stench of sweat and urine.

Katerina had been waiting for almost thirty minutes before the officer escorted Sir Rowland Deveraux into the room.

Deveraux waited for the guard to leave. 'And who might you be, young lady.'

'My name is Celeste Dupont, Sir Rowland and I'm here to help you.'

'Ah, French.'

She shook her head. 'Belgian.'

'I certainly would not be averse to being represented by such an attractive woman, Miss Dupont, but I already have excellent legal support.'

'I am not an ordinary lawyer, Sir Rowland. I specialise in human rights and have travelled from the Haig specifically to talk to you.' She picked up the F&M bag and placed it on the table. 'I also picked these up on my way here.' She took out the box of truffles and placed it in front of him.

Deveraux looked at the box then up at Katerina. 'Goodness me . . . you have done your homework. I simply adore these.'

'Yes I was told . . . But I have a confession to make.'

'A confession?'

She leaned forward. 'I had one in the taxi.'

He gave a little chuckle and opened the box. 'Would you care for another?'

'No thank you. You enjoy them.'

He took one of the truffles and held it under his nose. As he took in the aroma he said, 'Mmmm . . . amazing,' then put it in his mouth and licked his fingers.

Katerina watched as Deveraux savoured the confection.

A few moments later he said. 'That was wonderful. Now, Miss Dupont, what exactly is it you can do for me?'

Pentonville Prison an hour after Katerina left.

The whining alarm echoed off the cold stone walls of the old building. Inmates added to the cacophony with shrieks and profanities, as three officers ran up the metal stairs.

A guard knelt at Deveraux's side. 'Get the doctor!' he shouted as the officers rushed into the cell.

One of them bent down and checked for a pulse. A couple of seconds later he straightened up. 'No need to bother the doc . . . This bugger's gone.'

Another guard picked up the box of truffles. As he passed them round he said, 'Shame to let these go to waste lads.'

THE END